Torn Through Time

A Midshipman's Journey

LARRY W WADE

RED HERON
— PUBLISHING —

Published by Red Heron Publishing

Shepherdsville, Kentucky

Library of Congress Control Number: 2025918102

ISBN 979-8-9999109-1-2 (paperback)

ISBN 979-8-9999109-2-9 (hardback)

ISBN 979-8-9999109-0-5 (ebook)

Cover design by Larry W. Wade

Printed in the United States of America

To my wife and the rest of my family

> *for always encouraging me to keep going... even when maybe you should've told me to stop*

And to my Dad

> *whose stories about serving aboard a submarine sparked my imagination*

> *Blending your real-life experiences with my love of science fiction made this journey deeply personal*

CONTENTS

"Victory is never guaranteed. But honor is claimed in the moments a man stands alone, relying on strength and courage, knowing the price... and paying it anyway."

Admiral Alexander Bennett

CHAPTER 1

Helen Sinclair exited The Ritz-Carlton through the door held open by a young man in a crisp red doorman's uniform—just a touch too large on his slender frame. A cool, whispering breeze met her as she stepped onto the covered walkway, and she instinctively tucked a stray lock of black hair behind one ear. Offering the doorman a faint smile of thanks, she stepped into the Washington night. Her evening gown, elegant and sleeveless, left her arms exposed to the damp chill in the air. Goosebumps rose along her skin, and she folded her arms gently around herself.

As she descended the steps, the Bell Captain caught sight of her approach and lifted the radio clipped to his shoulder. With a practiced press of a button, he summoned her limousine. Straightening his uniform, he stepped out from behind his post just as the long, black vehicle emerged from the line of luxury cars and glided forward.

Years of routine allowed him to time his movements perfectly, arriving at her side the instant the limo eased to a graceful stop. With a polite nod, he opened the rear door and waited as she slid into the plush leather interior. Once she was seated, he closed the door with quiet precision.

In the glossy black finish of the limousine, his face flashed briefly, deep-lined and thoughtful, before it disappeared as the car merged with the late-night D.C. traffic. He pushed his cap back slightly, revealing a mop of short, curly white hair, and watched the limousine disappear down the slick street, its taillights muted in the misty air. His gaze drifted back to the young doorman still standing tall at the hotel's entrance, his posture rigid as though awaiting inspection. The Bell Captain allowed himself a faint smile at the earnestness of youth.

As he returned to his station, his thoughts wandered, as they often did, to the parade of guests who had passed through The Ritz-Carlton over the years. Movie stars, diplomats, political powerbrokers... some he recognized, many he didn't. Some were all flash and feathers, *popinjays*, as he liked to call them, hovering at the fringes of real influence. But others? Others held the levers of true power, the kind that didn't make headlines but shaped them.

Reaching his post, he glanced down at his guest list, then paused. His eyes lifted again to the now-empty street, narrowing in thought. *Who was that young woman? Movie star? Up-and-coming senator's aide? No,* he thought. *There was something different about her. Something composed, deliberate. Not a popinjay. Not her.*

Inside the limousine, Helen sank into the rich leather seat with a sigh of satisfaction. The events of the week, each one a step higher than the last, had led to this night. A night of success, of possibility, of unexpected emotion. Just when she thought she had reached the summit of her ambitions, life had surprised her again. It wasn't an unwelcome surprise. Just... a curve she hadn't seen coming.

She reached for the wispy silk wrap beside her and drew it across her bare shoulders, folding her arms once more, this time for warmth and comfort. Leaning back, she rested her head and let her eyes fall shut. The soft rhythm of streetlights filtered through the tinted windows, flickering gently across her face. Her thoughts drifted as the city glided past, and images from the past several days began to stir in her mind.

It had only been a week ago, she recalled, that she'd walked into the modest reception area outside the Secretary of the Navy's office...

***

"Good morning. May I help you?" the receptionist asked as Helen approached the desk.

"Good morning," Helen replied, setting her briefcase gently on the corner. "I'm Helen Sinclair. I have an appointment with the Secretary."

"He's expecting you, Ms. Sinclair." The receptionist offered a pleasant smile. "Please have a seat, and I'll let him know you're here."

Helen nodded her thanks and took a seat on the edge of one of the two button-tufted leather chairs beside a small round table. She had been to the Pentagon before, but its labyrinthine design never failed to disorient her. Its concentric rings and interlocking corridors made her feel like a mouse in a maze. She'd arrived early, knowing it was easy to get turned around—and in her business, being late to a meeting with the Secretary of the Navy was not an option.

The receptionist placed the phone back in its cradle and glanced over at Helen. *Prim, proper, and nervous as a cat,* she thought. "Ms. Sinclair, the Secretary will see you now," she said, still smiling and trying to put her at ease.

Helen stood, smoothing her skirt and blouse. She squared her shoulders and drew in a slow, calming breath. *This is it,* she thought. *These next few minutes could decide everything.*

She glanced at a framed portrait hanging on the wall. Her reflection stared back, faintly visible in the glass. She tucked a lock of hair behind her ear, watching as the tension slowly faded from the corners of her eyes. Feeling better, she realized she was looking at the smiling face of Benjamin Harris, the current Secretary of the Navy. *I hope he's still smiling by the time I leave,* she thought wryly.

Turning with renewed focus, Helen offered a confident smile to the receptionist and stepped toward the tall walnut door. She gripped the antique brass knob, paused to steel herself, and walked into the Secretary's office.

Two men stood as she entered. The Secretary and a familiar face beside him in uniform.

"Helen, thank you for making time on short notice," the Secretary began, then paused as Helen lifted a hand in polite dismissal and smiled.

"Mr. Secretary, no need for apologies. I understand your schedule is demanding. Thank you for inviting me."

She turned to the naval officer. She had recognized him immediately.

"Admiral, it's good to see you again," she said, a slight catch in her voice. At forty-five, he was the youngest Rear Admiral in U.S. naval history and arguably the most handsome. *Well, unofficially. But I'm sure the receptionist out front would agree,* she thought.

"Please, Helen. As we agreed, call me Jim. Otherwise, I'll be forced to call you Ms. Sinclair," he said with a warm smile and a hint of a twinkle in his eye.

For Pete's sake, how does he do that? she wondered. *Do all men have that ability or does it come with the uniform?*

Realizing she was staring, she caught herself. "No, please don't... Jim. I prefer Helen." She smiled as her cheeks flushed. Just in time, she turned back to the Secretary and caught the amused smile he quickly wiped from his face.

Damn it. Most important day of my career and I'm acting like I'm sixteen again.

The Secretary motioned toward a pair of antique leather chairs. Once they were seated, he leaned back in his own chair, regarding her silently. Helen shifted slightly under his scrutiny.

Then he leaned forward, planting both hands on the desk.

"Ms. Sinclair," he said formally. The shift in tone was unmistakable. The introductions were over. This was a man responsible for more than two million personnel and a budget north of $180 billion. He had no time for fluff.

"We've reviewed your proposal to outfit our submarines with your new stealth system. R&D pored over every detail. They provided me a summary and a recommendation."

Helen sat up straighter, barely breathing.

"They estimate your design improves stealth performance by eighty-five point six percent. Even under active enemy sonar."

A surge of excitement coursed through her.

"However," he continued, "they also noted that while the technology is promising, there's a significant risk it won't work. And it comes with a price tag... over five billion per boat for all seven active nuclear submarines."

He looked her squarely in the eyes. "That's a lot of money."

Helen's heart sank. Her vision blurred. "But Mr. Secretary... that level of improvement... it's worth the risk. I understand the cost, but surely the Navy..."

He raised his hands to cut her off. "Let me finish, Ms. Sinclair. I've decided the Navy can't afford to miss this opportunity—if it works. So, we'll install your system on one boat, the *USS Trumpetfish*. If it performs as projected, we'll take the next step."

He looked to the Admiral and grinned. "Jim was her captain before he put those stars on his collar."

His smile faded as he turned serious again. "Jim, would you walk Ms. Sinclair through the plan?"

Helen turned to the Admiral, trying to absorb the emotional whiplash.

"I've already spoken to Captain Morris," he began. "Old friend. I explained what we're doing to my boat... well, his boat now." He smiled at his own slip. "We'll keep the installation and testing tightly under wraps."

He stood and paced slowly, then turned to face her again.

"If this works, Helen, it could save lives. Thousands of them."

She met his eyes and nodded.

"So," the Secretary interrupted, drawing their attention, "how long will the install take?"

Helen's mind raced. *Equipment timelines, staffing, contingencies... no room for overpromising.* "Roughly eight months, Mr. Secretary. My team can handle most of the external modifications, but I'll need to be aboard during the final three months to integrate the system with the nuclear reactor. I'll also need to ride along during sea trials to monitor and adjust the system in real time."

The Secretary beamed. "Ms. Sinclair, bring in your team. The *Trumpetfish* is yours."

A wave of gratitude and validation hit her. Years of sacrifice—all for this moment.

"Thank you, Mr. Secretary. I promise your faith in me won't be misplaced."

She shook hands with both men, doing her best to suppress the irrepressible grin tugging at her lips.

"Congratulations, Ms. Sinclair," the Secretary said warmly, circling his desk to place a hand on her shoulder. "Oh, one more thing. We're hosting a banquet at The Ritz-Carlton this Friday. You and a few other contractors will be honored. My office will send the details."

She nodded graciously and turned to leave, the Admiral following close behind.

As they passed the receptionist's desk, he reached out and touched her elbow, sending a ripple of warmth up her arm.

"Ms. Sinclair... I mean Helen," he said in a low voice.

She turned, a small smile playing at her lips. "Yes, Jim?"

"I'd be honored to escort you to the banquet, unless you plan to invite someone else."

"No. No one." She winced slightly. "I mean, yes, I'd love that. Thank you."

"Great. I'll call tomorrow to sort out the details."

She smiled again, then noticed the receptionist now completely engrossed in her paperclips. *Fantastic,* Helen thought. *The gossip will beat me to the lobby.*

She turned to watch the Admiral return to the Secretary's office. *Beautiful man,* she mused. Then, catching the receptionist's sideways glance, she winked and tossed her a grin before striding out the door.

The limousine rolled up to the hotel entrance. The driver stepped out, opened the door, and waited. After a few moments, he peeked inside.

Helen was fast asleep in the back seat, arms folded gently around herself, a contented smile on her face.

CHAPTER 2

Helen gripped the chipped metal railing at the top of the staircase, gazing out over the hangar's sprawling interior. Cold white light poured down from overhead fixtures, illuminating a labyrinth of wiring harnesses, sensors, and control modules. All destined to become the core of the stealth system. Her stealth system.

Below, technicians moved with controlled urgency, weaving around components, scanning tags, and scribbling notes on their tablets. Every part had already passed rigorous quality inspections before arriving here. Once installed, each would be tested again.

Helen closed her eyes and tilted her head back, stretching to work out the stiffness in her neck. Tomorrow, a team from the Secretary of the Navy's office was scheduled to inspect the site, and she and her crew had been working nearly nonstop to make sure everything was ready.

It had been just over two months since the SecNav had given her the green light. Since then, this hangar had become her second home. A fortress of cables, consoles, and humming machines occupied one corner... along with an inflatable air mattress she'd collapsed onto more nights than she could count. But the sacrifice didn't bother her. This system was her creation. Under her leadership, a team of the sharpest minds in engineering, programming, and field operations was bringing it to life. But it didn't matter how many helped build it, this was her creation, her vision.

Helen had the kind of mind that saw systems the way an artist sees a finished painting. She could break down complexities, reassemble them in her mind, and predict how they'd perform in the real world. One of her professors had once said she viewed engineering the way Mozart saw music, as whole and alive, before a single note or line was laid down.

No one was surprised when she graduated early. But few expected her to drop out of MIT at seventeen, only two semesters in, to launch her own consulting firm.

She had no degree, no license, and no formal experience, but that hadn't stopped her. She hired credentialed engineers to validate her designs and affix their seals, and quickly, Sinclair Engineering Solutions became one of the most in-demand firms on the planet.

Her phone buzzed in her back pocket, startling her. She blinked and straightened, rubbing her tired eyes. Sleep-deprived and running on fumes, she fumbled for the phone and answered.

"Sinclair."

"Helen. It's good to hear your voice."

Her heart skipped a beat. She straightened instinctively. "Uhm... Hello, Admiral."

She cringed at the awkwardness in her tone, already feeling the warmth rising in her cheeks.

"It's Jim, remember?"

Her smile softened. "I remember. Hello, Jim."

"I'm riding herd on the inspection team that's coming in tomorrow," he said, then paused. "But I just landed, and I was wondering if you'd like to grab a drink."

Helen's eyes widened. "Jim, I... I'd love to, but..." She glanced up at the hangar's steel rafters, searching for a graceful way to say no. "I'm a mess. My hair's a disaster, I've been living in these coveralls, and I'm running on three hours of sleep. Maybe another time?"

"I'm still at the Jacksonville airport. It'll take me about an hour to grab my bag, pick up a car, and drive over. I'll meet you at The Palace Saloon on Centre Street. Say around nine? That gives you time to shed the coveralls."

For a beat, Helen hesitated. She hadn't been on a date in... well, she didn't care to finish that thought.

Screw it.

"Okay," she said. "I'll see you there."

She ended the call and looked down at the organized chaos below—the tangled cables, humming equipment, and ever-busy technicians. Then her eyes drifted to the sagging air mattress in the corner, the twisted sheets half-pooling onto the cold floor.

"Sorry, old friend," she murmured with a grin. "I just got a better offer."

*
**

Jim sat down at the bar and placed a foot on the brass footrail that ran the forty-foot bar's length. The old wooden chair creaked as he settled into it. He ran his hand along the heavily lacquered bar top and wondered briefly how many drinks had crossed this bar since it opened in 1903.

"Good evening, sir," said the bartender as he approached. "What can I get you?"

"Coffee for now, black. I'm meeting someone here for a drink and I just flew down from Pearl. I need a little something to shake loose the cobwebs."

The bartender paused when he heard the Naval base at Pearl Harbor mentioned. He slowly placed the coffeepot on the bar and snapped to attention before bellowing, "Officer on the Deck!"

Jim grimaced and glanced around the nearly empty bar. No one had even flinched at the bartender's outburst. He turned back to the bartender, who was smiling from ear-to-ear.

"Heh... heh... sorry, sir." The bartender chuckled softly as he resumed pouring the cup of coffee. "As retired-navy mine own self, I enjoy having a fellow swabbie in the place."

Jim reached out, taking the offered coffee mug, and blew across the steaming liquid. "Which ship did you serve on?" he asked the old barkeep.

"I was the COB on the Stonefish," he said with pride in his voice.

Jim looked at him carefully, analyzing the man in front of him. Slowly he leaned forward and in a quiet voice whispered, "Torpedoes are scary bastards, aren't they, Chief?"

He carefully watched the bartender's eyes as they widened considerably before narrowing into slits.

"I wouldn't know, sir," he said stiffly. "The Stonefish was never struck by a torpedo. You're thinking of a different ship."

"Oh yeah, that's right," Jim said smoothly as he leaned back in this chair and took a sip of the still scalding hot coffee. "It was a hurricane off the coast of Charleston. Now that I think about it."

"Yes, sir. That it was, sir." The bartender looked very uneasy.

Jim smiled and placed his cup back on the bar before standing up. Thrusting his shoulders back, he raised his hand to his brow in a stiff salute. He held the salute and waited until the dumbstruck bartender snapped to attention and returned the salute before lowering his arm. "Well done, Chief. You should be proud. You and your boys did a fine job out there... real fine."

As Jim returned to his chair, the bartender poured himself a cup of coffee and then reached under the bar and pulled out a bottle of rum. Jim watched as he added a dollop of the caramel-colored liquid to both their mugs. "Few people have even heard of the Stonefish, let alone know about the run-in we had with the... hurricane. What's your pay grade?" he asked as he placed the bottle on the bar.

Before Jim could answer, the door burst open and Helen strode in and looked around before spotting him at the bar.

"Admiral! I'm sorry I'm late," she gushed as she slid into the seat next to Jim and flashed both him and the bartender a broad smile.

The bartender looked at her and then looked at the Admiral as his eyes widened. Slowly, he tipped another jolt of the rum into his mug and took a slow sip.

Helen gazed at him quizzically and then looked at Jim giving him a "What's going on?" look. When Jim didn't respond, she shrugged and looked at his coffee mug. "Coffee?"

"Well," he grinned at her and gave the bartender a conspirator's wink. "There's coffee in there somewhere."

She grinned back and then looked over at the display of bottled beers behind the bar. "Could I have a bottle of Sam Adams Winter Lager?"

The bartender stared at her for a second and then glanced at Jim, who gave him a wink. Slowly, the smile returned to his face. He moved over to the beer refrigerator and retrieved a bottle. Walking back, he ignored the twist-off cap and popped off the cap using a bottle opener mounted to the bar. Placing a napkin on the bar, he put the bottle in front of her. "There you are, ma'am."

Helen reached for her purse just as Jim reached for his wallet, but the bartender waved them off. "It's on the house. You need anything else, you just yell for ol' Ben," he said with a wink and extended his hand to Jim. "Nice talking with you, Admiral, real nice."

Jim shook the man's hand and watched as the old submariner moved down to wait on a couple that had just arrived, giggling and laughing, at the far end of the bar.

"You two know each other?" Helen asked quizzically.

Jim turned his gaze back to Helen. "Oh, no. We just met." Jim glanced down the long bar and watched as the bartender engaged the new couple in conversation. "But we've sailed some of the same waters. That creates its own type of bond." Jim slid out of his chair and offered her his hand. "Why don't we grab a table?"

Helen picked up her beer bottle near the bottom, grabbing the napkin as well. Then she took his hand and let him lead her to a table that sat alongside the wall. "This is a fascinating place," she commented as she settled into the chair that he pulled out for her. The bar room was narrow but long. A row of tables sat directly across from the forty-foot-long bar, having only a narrow aisle separating them. Above the tables, murals decorated the walls. The well-worn bar itself was unique in its size and its overhead gas lights provided a soft, warm glow that accented the wood's warmth.

"Yeah, it's a combination Navy slash biker bar." He glanced around the small room where the long bar, once again, drew his attention. "This place has seen its share of history. They say that Adolphus Busch, the founder of Anheuser-Busch, helped design the bar." He turned back to Helen and found her gazing at him and not at the bar.

"Fascinating," she said, not taking her eyes from his. She smiled at his clear unease as he stumbled out his agreement. *Not every day you make an Admiral blush,* she thought with smug satisfaction. She giggled and reached out to touch his elbow. He returned her serene smile and then steered the conversation into the safe areas of current affairs and the

Navy's current state. Ben came over carrying a tray filled with a plate of appetizers and a bottle of chardonnay, complete with two glasses, while they were talking.

"Not the best vintage in the world, but it's the best we've got."

Helen reached over and placed her hand on his as he sat the food tray on the table. "It's perfect. Thank you," she said and gave his hand a little squeeze.

Color rushed to his face and he cleared his throat noisily. "Uh... you're very welcome," he finally rasped. "Listen," he said as he leaned conspiratorially toward Helen and pitched his voice to a low growl, "if this old sea dog here gives you any trouble, you just let me know. Alright?"

"I'll do that, Ben."

As he left, Jim leaned forward and smiled. "I think he likes you."

Helen regarded Jim thoughtfully. She took in his blue eyes, his close-cropped brown hair, the five o'clock shadow that outlined his chiseled features. "Should we be doing this? I mean, will you get in trouble?" she asked quietly.

"Why would I get in trouble for having drinks with a beautiful woman? I'm in the Navy. Hell, a submariner at that. They'll probably give me a medal." He laughed as he took a sip of his wine.

"But isn't this a conflict of interest? I mean, tomorrow you're bringing in a team to evaluate the progress of my program and here we are having drinks in a bar." She said, with a bit of exasperation in her voice.

"Don't forget the cheese sticks. We also have cheese sticks."

"I'm being serious!"

"OK, OK. No, it's not a conflict of interest. First, yes, I'm bringing a team in tomorrow. But no, I'm not on the team. I'm just the liaison between a third-party audit and the SecNav." He took a cheese stick and dipped it into the small bowl of marinara sauce. He took a bite and then pointed at her with the half-eaten cheese stick. "Second, I've tied my wagon to yours. I've gone on record to say that I have full confidence in your system and you. Your success is my success. That's why we brought in a company outside the Navy for the audit. It had to be someone that would not be afraid to give an honest report." He popped the other end of the cheese stick in his mouth. "Well, what do you say to that?" He challenged her.

Helen smiled and picked up a cheese stick, and dipped it into the sauce. "Well, you have ethics... and you're not a double-dipper." She took a small bite and then pointed the cheese stick at him and winked. "Both traits that I admire in a man."

Ben leaned back against the counter behind the bar and watched as they loosened up and started relaxing with each other. *Cute couple,* he thought as he picked up a small towel and started wiping down the bar. He looked up briefly and saw Jim reach over and take her hand. *Yep, a really cute couple.*

CHAPTER 3

"Outrageous!" China's Director-General of International Affairs thundered, slamming his hand against the polished conference table. The sharp crack echoed through the room, punctuating the fury etched into his features. He sneered at the ambassadors from Great Britain, Germany, and Russia.

"For generations, America has acted as if it stands above the rest of the world. But this latest provocation... this insult... is beyond tolerance." His voice dropped to a growl. "We should not continue forcing our nations to endure their insufferable arrogance. They believe their obsession with technological progress and the pursuit of wealth makes them superior to those cultures that honor tradition and the old ways."

He spat the final word like it burned his tongue. "Americans view us as primitive. As uncivilized." He paused, collecting himself with a deep breath. "Gentlemen, we can neither ignore nor forgive this most recent act of aggression."

"And just what exactly do you mean by that?" asked a sharply dressed man in a finely tailored pinstriped suit. His thick English accent left no doubt about his identity, even though everyone in the room already knew it. He represented Great Britain.

Director-General Wei Cheng met the ambassador's gaze unflinchingly. Then he turned, scanning the expressions of the Russian and German ambassadors. They both avoided his eyes.

Cowards, he thought coldly. *Their governments have already pledged their loyalty to the alliance, yet they lack the courage to speak.*

Returning his attention to the British ambassador, Wei offered a smile laced with contempt. "Surely your government sees what the rest of the world already understands. America is no longer the global power it once was." He waved a hand dismissively, as if brushing away a tired myth. "We are offering your nation the opportunity to stand with us, to show the United States that we are no longer subservient to its whims and pressures."

The British ambassador glowered at them, then slowly rose to his feet. He leaned forward, placing both hands on the table, his face just inches from Wei's.

"The United States is our most steadfast ally," he said in a low, deliberate voice. "And I will not take part in any conversation that maligns its name."

He straightened to his full height and adjusted his tie with calm precision. "This meeting is over."

With a swift motion, he pulled on his overcoat and made his way to the door. His hand grasped the knob, but he paused, glancing back over his shoulder.

"Be advised," he said, his tone like steel, "Great Britain will not tolerate any action taken against the United States. Should you choose that path, you will face consequences... severe ones. And trust me, gentlemen, you do not want the Crown as your enemy."

Without another word, he opened the door and exited.

Director-General Wei's face darkened with rage as the door clicked shut. *Insufferable fool. You presume to lecture me?*

His hands clenched and unclenched, his fury barely contained. He glanced toward one of his security officers and gave a single sharp nod.

The agent gave an almost imperceptible nod in return and lifted his shoulder slightly, speaking quietly into the microphone hidden in his collar. Outside, the black sedan parked at the curb shifted into gear and eased into traffic behind the ambassador's limousine.

Back inside the conference room, Wei slipped on his coat and pulled his gloves tight over his fingers.

"While disappointing," he said calmly, "I anticipated the ambassador's response."

The agent at the door tapped his earpiece, listening. He stepped closer to the Director-General and whispered something into his ear. Wei listened, his expression unreadable—until a slow, satisfied smile spread across his face. He flexed his gloved fingers, savoring the smooth texture of the leather.

"Inform your governments," he said, turning to the remaining ambassadors, "that our plans will proceed as scheduled." He walked to the doorway, then paused and glanced back at the men still seated in silence.

"Oh, and by the way," he added casually, "I've just been informed that our British friend was involved in a tragic accident on his way to the embassy."

He let that hang in the air for a moment longer, then stepped through the doorway and disappeared.

*
**

In secret, China, Russia, and Germany formed the Phoenix Alliance, a coalition built on the shared goal of ending what they called the unjust dominance of the world's lone superpower. Publicly, they spoke of restoring their nations to former greatness. Privately, they were preparing for war.

The first step was economic. Under the radar, each member nation began building vast strategic oil reserves, quietly shifting their economies to a wartime footing. It was subtle, but it didn't go unnoticed. Oil prices surged. Gasoline costs in the United States climbed to record highs. Wall Street analysts blamed the spike on China's booming economy, interpreting it as a temporary imbalance that OPEC would soon correct with increased production quotas.

But the markets were wrong.

After a year of covert mobilization, the Phoenix Alliance launched the opening move of its global campaign. German forces stormed and captured Ramstein Air Base in western Germany, a major hub for the U.S. Air Force. The attack came without warning, swift and devastating. The fighting ended within hours, with minimal casualties. Within four hours of seizing the base, a flight of twenty-three aircraft lifted off from its runways. Among them were nineteen American C-130 Hercules from the 37th Airlift Squadron and four F-15E Strike Eagles on loan from the 48th Fighter Wing. All of them were now under German control.

The aircraft flew eastward into Russian airspace and eventually landed in Tiksi. There, the C-130s were refueled and loaded with Russian armored vehicles and hundreds of infantry troops. Chinese soldiers, who had crossed into Russia earlier that day through a sympathetic North Korea, joined them.

Led by the F-15Es, the aircraft flew over the Bering Sea under the guise of standard American military flights. Their destination was Elmendorf Air Force Base in Alaska.

Elmendorf's radar systems tracked them the entire way. But the deception worked. No alerts were sounded. Instead, base personnel made calls up the chain of command, assuming a breakdown in communication was to blame for the unscheduled inbound flights.

No one suspected anything until it was far too late.

The first wave of GBU-39 GPS-guided bombs struck the troop barracks, annihilating most of the base's personnel in seconds. The targeting was precise. It was deadly to American forces while sparing most of the infrastructure. Within minutes, the C-130s landed, their rear ramps dropping before the wheels even stopped turning. Russian and Chinese troops stormed the base. What remained of Elmendorf's defenders offered scattered resistance, but they were quickly overrun.

Word of Elmendorf's fall reached Phoenix Alliance command, and within hours, they escalated the conflict again, this time on a global scale.

A missile launched from German territory arced silently through the upper atmosphere. It carried a single Russian-made nuclear warhead. Its target was predetermined.

It struck London.

The city was obliterated.

There were no survivors. The British capital was reduced to ash and irradiated ruin. It would be generations before anything would live there again.

The nuclear strike sent shockwaves through the world. It was not just the destruction that shook the global order, but the message behind it. The Phoenix Alliance's military commander issued a statement as part of their formal declaration of war:

> "We regret the necessity of using a nuclear weapon. However, in our struggle to cast off the oppressive yoke of the United States, we cannot allow any allied strongholds to exist on our doorstep. This is America's fight. Any nation that offers aid to the United States will be treated as an enemy and dealt with accordingly. We will not hesitate to use nuclear weapons again. However, if the United States refrains from employing its nuclear arsenal,

we too shall abstain from further nuclear action in this righteous war."

The threat had its intended effect.

Allied nations that had once stood firmly beside the United States withdrew their support. Diplomats severed ties. U.S. bases across the globe were shuttered, their personnel isolated. America was alone.

In just four months, Alaska, Washington, and Oregon had fallen under Phoenix Alliance control. Northern California burned with scattered resistance, but the front line was inching southward by the day. The invasion was no longer a warning. It was a full-scale war for the future of American soil.

CHAPTER 4

Eighteen years later, President James Conner sat behind his desk in the Oval Office. His wire-framed glasses balanced precariously at the end of his nose as he scanned his morning briefing. Scowling at what he read, he tossed the report to the far corner of his desk and rubbed his temples just as his secretary's voice came over the intercom.

"Mr. President?"

He frowned and pressed the intercom button. "Yes, Janet?"

"Sir, Mr. Conrad is here."

"OK, send him in."

The door opened, and Thomas Conrad, his Chief of Staff, strode past a Secret Service agent and into the room. The agent quietly closed the door behind him.

"Good morning, Mr. President," Thomas said, dropping into one of the chairs in front of the desk.

"Unless you're reading a different briefing, I don't know how you can say that," the President muttered.

Thomas paused, pulling a folder from his briefcase. "No, sir. Same briefing. And no, there's nothing good about it."

President Conner swiveled his chair toward the wall of photographs. His eyes landed on the worn image of President Tim Brenner. *That must've been near the end of his term,* he thought. *This job ages people—and Brenner wasn't exactly built for pressure.*

He stood and waved a hand toward the portraits. "Take a look, Thomas. These are the men who put us in this position." He stopped in front of Brenner's photo.

"Sixty-two percent."

"Excuse me?"

"Brenner's approval rating. Two years into his term, before the war started, he was sitting at sixty-two percent. Then came the attack. His inability to lead caused massive losses. The West Coast, from the Rockies to the Texas panhandle—gone. And it wasn't until his generals took the reins that we stopped the bleeding. By the time the election rolled around, his approval was twenty-two percent. Sergio Reyes crushed him."

Conner's gaze shifted to Reyes' photo registering the piercing eyes, confident smile.

"He ran on peace," the President said, tapping the frame. "Told the country that international pressure would force the Phoenix Alliance to back off. Thought diplomacy would bring Alaska and the West Coast back without more bloodshed."

He snorted. "Fool. When you've got a bull by the tail and kicking it in the ass, you don't worry about world opinion."

Thomas stepped beside him. "Well, he was re-elected. The people believed he was doing the right thing."

"They believed it because they wanted to. America was desperate for peace. And Reyes wasn't evil… just naive. But a President doesn't get to be naive. He kept chasing a resolution that was always just out of reach." Conner returned to his desk. "At the end of his first term, he had nothing. But right before the election, a supposed breakthrough in peace talks shot him back up in the polls. He made promises, painted a hopeful picture, and it worked. He got four more years." He looked again at the photo. "Eight years. Nothing to show for it."

Thomas nodded solemnly.

Then Conner's attention turned to the next photo of President Borland. "Now this one…" He reached up, took the picture off the wall, and held it up. "After eight years of Reyes, the country still could've recovered—if it hadn't elected this clown." He flung the photo across the room. Glass shattered as it hit the wall and fell to the floor. "He nearly destroyed us with his isolationist garbage!"

Thomas walked over and picked up the broken frame, careful to avoid the glass. He studied Borland's face. The eyes looked distant. Or was that just his own frustration projecting? He set the frame on a nearby table. The staff would have it repaired and rehung by morning.

"James," Thomas said quietly, "rehashing the past won't solve today's problems. We need to focus on moving forward."

Conner didn't respond right away. He stared out the window, lost in mcmory. Borland had halted all international trade, hoping to crash the global economy and force the Phoenix Alliance back to the negotiating table. And they came back, all right—after America's economy crumbled. Conner could still hear the laughter that probably followed behind closed doors. Borland's approval rating had plummeted into the teens just a week before the election. His loss seemed certain. Then came the intercepted message.

A communique from the Chinese ruling family to Phoenix Alliance leadership. It urged a quick resolution that would allow them to return the occupied regions, allowing China to gain favor with the world. The letter blamed the effectiveness of the U.S. embargo for causing widespread famine in China and Russia. When this was released to the public, the narrative changed overnight. The nation cheered. Borland was re-elected in a landslide.

But it had all been a lie.

That message had been a calculated deception—designed to manipulate the American election and keep a weak President in power. Two months ago, during Conner's own campaign, another message had been intercepted. This time, it was real.

"... Proceed with the plan to inform your American counterparts that an agreement is not only possible soon, but probable. It is imperative that they believe this. Only if this deception works will we prevent James Conner from obtaining the Presidency of the United States. We cannot allow him and his warmongering mentality to take power.

Our plans are too near completion to permit any disruption at this juncture. We must continue to influence the elections to avoid an all-out war until we are ready..."

When the American public saw that, the illusion shattered. For years, they had chased the hope of peace like a carrot on a stick. Always just out of reach. Always promising something better. Before the leak, Conner had polled at thirty-two percent. His blunt rhetoric and military background had turned off voters who still clung to the dream of diplomacy. One campaign speech had started with, "Elect me and I'll kick the bastards out of America." It got applause, but not from everyone. Then the message broke. His approval shot to ninety-three percent. He won in a landslide.

Now, two months into his presidency, James Conner sat behind the same desk where his predecessors had made decisions that shaped history. He wondered if, one day, another President would sit here, look up at his photo, and call him a fool.

He turned to Thomas and motioned to the chair across from his desk. They sat in silence for a moment until Conner broke it.

"How's the troop buildup in Colorado coming?" His voice was low and tired. He leaned forward, elbows on the desk, head in his hands. When Thomas didn't immediately answer, he looked up. "Well?"

Thomas measured his response. "It's progressing, sir. As well as it can. The previous administrations cut troop numbers and scaled back equipment to show good faith during negotiations."

Conner slammed a hand on the desk. "Tell me something I don't know."

Thomas nodded slightly and clasped his hands. "Despite the cuts, the personnel we have are some of the most dedicated we've ever seen. After Borland gutted the defense budget, only the most committed stayed in uniform. And with the public finally waking up, enlistment is surging. The academies are also reporting one of the strongest graduating classes in years."

Conner leaned back, allowing a faint smile to form. "That's something, at least."

"I thought you'd like that, sir," Thomas said, smiling. The President's love for the Naval Academy was well known. "Maybe I should visit the academies. What do you think?"

Thomas nodded toward a bronze submarine statue on the bookshelf. "Why not start with the Naval Academy?"

Conner grinned. "My thoughts exactly." He hadn't been back to Annapolis since graduation. The idea stirred something nostalgic and steadying in him.

President Conner waved his aide away as he shrugged into his suit coat. As he fastened the top button and adjusted his tie, the aide picked up the President's briefcase and followed him towards the door at a respectful distance. Marine One had just landed on the South Lawn waiting to take the President to visit the Naval Academy in Annapolis. Without warning, the door flew open and Thomas Conrad burst in.

"Mr. President! We have a situation."

The President turned to his aide and gave a slight nod to the door. The aide quickly set the President's briefcase down next to one of Oval Office's sofas and quietly exited, closing the door behind her.

"OK, Thomas. What going on?"

"Sir, we've kept a close eye on Voyennyy Port in Northern Russian ever since one of their nuclear submarines, stationed there for months, suddenly went missing from our satellite's surveillance. That was three days ago. About an hour ago, one of our hydroacoustic sensors picked up an anomaly off the coast of Greenland. We can't be sure, but it could be the missing nuclear sub."

The President stared at his Chief of Staff and then slowly lowered himself to sit on the sofa's arm. "In all these years, they've been very vocal about their desire to keep this from becoming a nuclear war. Why would they suddenly decide to change their minds now?"

"With all due respect, sir. You are what's changed. America elected a military President and I think you are being tested. They want to know how will you respond to a nuclear threat." Thomas walked over to a side table and leaned against it. "James," he whispered. "It's a Stinger class submarine. Russia's newest nuclear sub. It's small but carries up to ten nuclear missiles on board, and it's quiet. Deadly quiet. If they didn't want us to know they were there, we wouldn't."

Reaching down, the President picked up his briefcase and rose slowly. He paused for a moment before giving his Chief of Staff a small smile that didn't quite reach his eyes. "Well, I guess it's our move. Let's send one of our ballistic missile submarines towards the East China Sea. If they back off, so will we."

"Yes sir, Mr. President. I'll make the call." Thomas said as the President opened the door.

"And Thomas."

"Yes, Mr. President?"

"Tell our sub to drag a string of cans behind them. Nice and loud. I want to make sure they hear us coming."

"Yes sir! Mr. President," Thomas smiled as he followed the President out of the Oval Office. *Damn right,* he thought. *About time that America wiped the blood off her lip and squared her shoulders.*

CHAPTER 5

Helen stepped up out of the hatch at the top of the submarine's conning tower, the cold air rushing to meet her face in sharp contrast to the stifling heat below. A bead of perspiration trickled down her temple, and she wiped it away with the sleeve of her jumpsuit. The fresh sea air felt like a gift... bracing, alive, and unfiltered.

She arched her back with a long, deliberate stretch, every vertebra in her spine cracking in protest after long hours hunched in the control bay. Letting out a tired breath, she stepped forward and leaned against the railing, eyes scanning the endless sweep of ocean. Despite the relief of fresh air and open space, she couldn't shake the uneasy feeling that always clung to her when she looked down at the vessel.

The Valkyrie-class submarine stretched before her like a sleeping leviathan. Its black hull shimmered with moisture, blending seamlessly with the dark sea surrounding it. For three months, she had seen this same view, day after day, night after night, as her team worked through the final installation of the stealth system. And yet, each time, the sight still gave her a chill. The submarine was a predator. There was no warmth in its design, no softness in its lines. It was built to vanish into the abyss, to stalk unseen. And thanks to her, it was about to become even more dangerous.

She placed a hand on the steel hull, its surface cool beneath her palm. Though it lay silent and still in the water, she could almost picture the intricate network of systems beneath the surface, quietly humming in standby: hydraulics pressurized, power routed, circuits alive with quiet potential. She imagined the faint pulse of electronics, the gentle stir of coolant through narrow pipes, and the soft readiness of the reactor holding steady. It wasn't moving, not yet, but in her mind, it was very much alive. Waiting. Poised to slip beneath the surface and vanish into the depths with quiet, lethal intent.

"Ms. Sinclair?" The uneven voice behind her startled her out of her ruminations. She turned slightly and looked over her shoulder at the young man's head poking up out of the hatch behind her.

Ugh, she thought to herself; *he looks more like twelve than the eighteen years required to join the Navy. And that squeaky voice isn't helping him.*

"Yes, Kevin?" she asked and gave him a small, tired smile.

"Would you like some tea, Ma'am?"

Helen smiled faintly. The young steward, Kevin, had been assigned to her since day one. Somewhere along the way, he had become something between a personal assistant and a shadow. Every time she turned around, he was there, always discreet, respectful, and surprisingly helpful. She had taken to calling him her "man Friday," though never to his face.

"Yes, Kevin," she said, her voice warm with fatigue. "That would be lovely."

With a final look at the waves crashing against the hull, she followed Kevin back down the steel ladder, the clang of the hatch sealing behind them echoing faintly in her ears.

As they made their way through the tight passageways, crewmen instinctively pressed themselves against the bulkheads to allow her through. The sub was alive with motion, men moving with practiced ease despite the confined quarters. The scent of machine oil and salt hung heavy in the air, and Helen found herself cataloging every sound, every glance. She didn't just feel like a guest here anymore. She felt like part of the machine.

Submariners had their own kind of family that was closer than most blood ties. You couldn't serve in a steel tube under hundreds of feet of ocean with people and not form bonds. She understood that now. It wasn't just the pressure from outside the hull that made a crew fuse together. It was the shared trust, the certainty that when things went wrong, the man or woman next to you wouldn't falter.

"Ms. Sinclair," said a short, broad-shouldered man rising from one of the tables as she entered. "Would you care to join me?"

Captain Morris nodded toward the seat across from his. His expression was neutral but polite, a formality born more of duty than friendship. Still, she appreciated the gesture.

Helen returned his nod and eased into the offered seat. Kevin stepped past her and retrieved a cup, gently placing a tea bag inside. He poured hot water from a pure white porcelain teapot, the steam curling upward in delicate spirals. Then he set the mug in front of her along with a small creamer, a neatly folded linen napkin, and a polished silver spoon for stirring.

Realizing his job was complete and she was in good hands, Kevin stood at attention near the end of the table.

"Permission to leave, sir?" he asked.

The captain nodded once. Kevin relaxed slightly, flashed Helen a proud smile, then slipped out of the wardroom with quiet efficiency.

The Captain turned back to Helen, studying her with an appraising gaze. When he was first informed that a new prototype stealth system would be installed on his submarine, he had taken it in stride. Modifications were nothing new. But three months ago, when he learned that the system's lead designer, now sitting calmly across from him, would personally oversee the final installation, he hadn't been able to hide his surprise. It wasn't that she was a woman. He had served alongside exceptional women throughout his career. It was her youth that gave him pause. She looked more like a graduate student than someone entrusted with cutting-edge military technology.

As if sensing his scrutiny, Helen looked up over the rim of her mug and locked her electric blue eyes on him. She took a slow sip of tea, then gently set the cup back on the table and gave him her full attention. Misreading the Captain's thoughtful silence, she spoke calmly.

"The installation is nearly complete, Captain. I'd say we'll finish in another twenty-four hours."

The Captain offered a slight smile, his thoughts drifting back to the day she first walked into his office. She had been striking. Tall, maybe five-nine, slim build, with those sharp, penetrating eyes that gave her a look of confidence well beyond her years. Still, his reaction hadn't been favorable. He had glanced from her to the Admiral who accompanied her, catching the look in the Admiral's eyes and feeling a flicker of unease. Romance was fine, in theory, but not when it involved his submarine.

Back then, she hadn't seemed like the kind of person who belonged in a weapons lab, let alone on a warship. But then he'd watched her get to work. Watched her snap on a tool belt, shoulder her way into a tight engine compartment, and tell seasoned mechanics to move aside. She'd done it without arrogance, just with an assurance that said she knew what she was doing.

And she did.

Within days, she'd won over the crew and, eventually, won over him too. She was young, yes, but brilliant, tough, and absolutely unflinching in the face of pressure. *No wonder the Admiral had fallen for her.*

"Very good, Ms. Sinclair," he said at last. "Once you and your team are finished, we'll head out and begin the sea trials. The Admiral and the SecNav are both eager to see how this experiment performs."

His tone darkened slightly as he spoke the last sentence, and he turned his gaze from her to the plaque on the wall.

Mounted beneath the gleaming submariner's dolphins was a brass plate etched with the name Trumpetfish.

She was a Valkyrie-class attack submarine, boasting four torpedo tubes and twelve vertical launch systems. She carried a full complement of Mk 48 ADCAP torpedoes and Tomahawk cruise missiles. With her nuclear reactor, she could stay submerged for months at a time, surfacing only when they needed to restock the food supplies.

She was quiet. Lethal. Built for deep-sea war.

And if Sinclair's new system worked as promised, she wouldn't just be silent, she'd be invisible. Free to roam anywhere in the world, undetected, with deadly purpose.

If it worked.

CHAPTER 6

Thirty-six hours later, Helen followed the Captain into the submarine's war room and stood slightly behind and to his left as he addressed the assembled officers.

"Good afternoon," the Captain said, letting his gaze pass over the gathered crew. "Now that we are at sea, I can fully brief you on the newly installed system. I know there has been a lot of speculation, and I regret that I've had to keep you in the dark until now. As you know, it has always been my policy that you are fully informed of anything pertaining to the submarine. However, due to the classified nature of this system, the higher-ups made it clear that no information was to be shared until we were underway. Even those who assisted with the installation have not been told its full purpose."

A glance around the room confirmed that he had their complete attention.

"Miss Sinclair's team has outfitted the Trumpetfish with a new stealth system," he continued. "This system uses a revolutionary design, and all information related to it is top secret. Only the highest-ranking officials in the military have been briefed on these sea trials."

"Excuse me, sir." A young officer raised his hand, his finger extended to catch the Captain's attention.

"Speak up, Andrew," the Captain said, giving him the floor.

"Well, sir, it's just that, well..." The young man blushed, clearly realizing he had just interrupted a formal briefing.

"Spit it out," the Captain encouraged. "If you've got something to say, let's hear it."

"Sir, the Trumpetfish is already the most silent submarine in the world. It just seems like a new stealth system wouldn't be necessary. No one can hear us now unless we want them to."

The Captain listened, noting the low murmur of agreement spreading through the room.

"Well said, Andrew," he replied, suppressing a smile as the officer flushed with relief. "But before we judge the value of the new system, let's hear more about it. Gentlemen, for those of you who haven't met her during her time aboard the Trumpetfish, allow me to introduce the designer of the system, Ms. Helen Sinclair."

There was no applause as Helen stepped forward, just the watchful eyes of the crew. She saw a few familiar faces but not many. Most of her time had been spent with those directly involved in the installation, and even then, she had been careful to avoid conversations that might reveal too much.

"Thank you, Captain," she said, offering him a brief nod before turning her attention to the room. "The system installed on the Trumpetfish is not simply the next iteration in quieting technology."

Puzzled expressions met her statement. Helen allowed the moment to settle before continuing.

"I didn't design this to reduce the submarine's sonar signature or to dampen its noise. This system will make the Trumpetfish vanish."

Disbelief rippled through the room. Some frowned. Others whispered to one another. Helen pressed forward before the room could erupt.

"Current systems use hull materials to absorb sonar, minimize machinery noise, and shape the vessel to reduce detectability. These methods help, but they're not perfect. In shallow water or close quarters, their effectiveness diminishes. And when we reduce our speed to remain undetected, we give up tactical advantage."

She paused to take a sip from the glass of water on the lectern. The room had gone silent. "This new system will make the Trumpetfish undetectable."

Gasps spread across the room, quickly silenced when the Captain raised his hand.

"I know what I've said is hard to believe," Helen continued, stepping out from behind the lectern to engage the officers directly. "Let me explain how it works. A semi-conductive gas called Ununoctium travels through the reactor core, where it's irradiated by the nuclear material. This exposure charges the gas and turns it highly magnetic. Pumps then force it out through thousands of tiny orifices in the hull.

Special contacts embedded in the hull attract the gas, forming a second skin less than a millimeter thick. That's what the wiring harnesses you've seen routed throughout the interior support. These contacts use the reactor's power to generate a strong magnetic field that holds the gas in place, then constantly adjust the polarity to make it flow like a river along the hull."

Helen made eye contact with each section of the room.

"This gas, once irradiated, conducts sound much like copper conducts electricity. When sonar pings the submarine, the gas carries that sound around the hull and sends it off in the same direction, completely undisturbed. Even returning echoes from nearby objects are redirected around us. To the enemy, it's as if we're not there."

She reached back and took another sip of water.

"It doesn't stop there. Internal noise, the kind we create just by operating the vessel, is absorbed and dissipated in the same way. And since the gas coats every external surface, including the propellers, it also eliminates the cavitation signature created when vacuum bubbles collapse along its blades. With this gas absorbing that energy, those sounds, that identifiable acoustic footprint... disappears.

A hand rose in the back.

"Yes?" Helen asked.

"Ma'am, are you saying our propulsion system won't leave any acoustic signal? What about the wake created by our movement through the water?"

Helen smiled. "The gas absorbs the sound generated as the propellers slice through the water. As the water leaves the blades, the sound waves are absorbed and redirected.

This system allows us to operate at full speed and maneuver freely while remaining absolutely silent." She could see the realization dawning across their faces.

"Now that I've given you a basic overview of the system's operation, I'll open the floor to questions."

Behind her, the Captain grinned as nearly every hand in the room shot into the air.

* * *

Hours later, the Captain leaned back into his chair in the cramped confines of his stateroom and gestured for Helen to make herself comfortable. The room was small and functional, like most of the submarine's interior. A narrow table folded down from the wall, flanked by two built-in bench seats that barely allowed room to stretch one's legs. A single bunk was tucked tightly into one corner—an upgrade from the triple-occupancy quarters elsewhere aboard. His desk and chair took up most of the remaining space. The only personal touch was a thin blue carpet, worn but clean, softening the hard metal floor beneath their feet.

Helen slid sideways onto one of the benches and leaned her back against the wall, pulling her legs up slightly and folding her hands in her lap.

"That was quite a speech out there," the Captain said as she settled in, his voice calm but tinged with admiration.

Helen rubbed at her tired eyes and gave him a faint, crooked grin. "That's quite a crew you've got, Captain. I haven't been grilled that hard since... well, honestly, I don't think I've *ever* been grilled like that."

"They're the best I've ever served with," he replied. He paused for a moment, listening to the low, steady hum of the ship around them. Then, more cautiously, he continued. "You know, this was the Admiral's sub before it was mine. These were his quarters. That's how far back we go."

Helen's eyebrows lifted slightly, surprised by the personal turn in the conversation.

"It's a hard life, being out here," the Captain continued. "Long stretches away from family and friends. You sacrifice a lot for this kind of duty. But being an Admiral? That's a different rhythm. A little more room for a personal life outside the service."

Helen's head lifted, and she felt heat rise in her cheeks. *So, he did know.* "I guess that means you've figured out that Jim... I mean, the Admiral... and I have been spending time together," she said cautiously, watching his expression.

The Captain didn't answer right away. Instead, he reached forward and pressed a button on the wall-mounted intercom. "Could I get two cups of black coffee brought to my stateroom?" he asked. A muffled acknowledgment crackled back through the speaker.

Turning back to her, he spoke softly. "Jim and I have been friends a long time. When I accepted command of the Trumpetfish, he was already waiting at the gangplank. I still think that if he'd had even a sliver of doubt about how I'd treat his boat, he might've tossed me overboard then and there."

Helen chuckled quietly and caught the glint of fondness in his eye. It was more than respect. It was a story wrapped in deep friendship.

"His feelings for you were obvious the first time I saw the two of you together," the Captain said, his gaze steady. "At first, I questioned why he'd let the Trumpetfish be the testbed for a project this ambitious. Jim is cautious. He doesn't gamble with lives. But now I get it. He trusts you. And after seeing you in action, so do I."

Helen felt herself flush again. "I... I don't really know what to say," she murmured.

"You don't need to say anything," he said with a small, reassuring nod.

A soft smile pulled at her lips. "He's a good man. The past few months have been a whirlwind. Getting the approvals, fighting for the project... and then Jim." Her voice trailed off, full of unspoken memories and private moments.

The Captain smiled at her gently. "Well, when we get back to port, you and Jim are going to have dinner with me and my wife. Jim might outrank me in uniform, but at my dinner table, twenty-six years of marriage gives me all the authority I need to keep him in line."

Helen laughed, grateful for the moment of lightness. It felt like the first time in days that the weight of her work and the burden of secrecy had lifted. If only a little.

CHAPTER 7

When the noon bell rang, Tony slammed his Nuclear Physics book shut and stuffed it into his bag with more force than necessary. He stepped into the hallway, intent on getting some air and maybe clearing his head. He hadn't made it more than a few paces when a hand clamped down on his shoulder.

Already irritated, Tony spun around, jaw tight.

"Where the hell is Brent?" Reid demanded. His cheeks were flushed red, whether from anger or embarrassment, Tony couldn't tell. "He's screwing us on this project!"

Exactly what I want to know, Tony thought. *But damned if he was going to let anyone come after Brent without going through him first.*

"He's busy," Tony snapped. "So back off."

Reid blinked, surprised by the intensity in Tony's voice. He took a half-step back, momentarily silenced. At the Academy, it was never a good idea for a plebe to antagonize a firstie, especially not Tony Hendricks. Tony's reputation for leadership, performance, and sheer physical presence made him a formidable figure even among his peers.

The United States Naval Academy classified all students as midshipmen, but their titles also reflected their year. Freshmen were fourth-class midshipmen called plebes. Sophomores were third-class and referred to as youngsters. Juniors were second-class, and finally, seniors were first-class midshipmen, known simply as firsties.

Reid, a plebe, had been placed on a special project team with Tony and Brent due to his outstanding performance in computer science. The brass hoped pairing him with the Academy's two top engineering students would elevate his social and teamwork skills. So far, results were mixed.

Reid exhaled and looked down at his shoes, clearly biting back another retort.

"Sorry, Tony," he muttered, still staring at what looked like an imaginary scuff mark on his otherwise immaculate shoes. Then he glanced up, determination returning. "I'm just... damn it, Tony. You know the pressure I'm under. I'm in over my head, trying to keep up with the top two midshipmen in the Academy. If I screw this up, I'll be lucky to get assigned to a mop bucket, let alone a command."

Tony softened slightly. *Reid wasn't wrong. The kid had talent, but no one expected him to carry the team. That was Brent's job and Tony's. And Brent's absence was screwing all of them.*

Tony placed a reassuring hand on Reid's shoulder. "You know Brent and I aren't going to let you fail," he said, cracking a grin. "The top two midshipmen at Annapolis can't exactly have a project go down in flames, can we?"

Reid managed a grin in return. His tension melted away a little.

"Thanks, Tony. I appreciate that."

He turned and disappeared down the corridor, his earlier frustration replaced with a little more confidence.

Now that Reid's squared away, Tony thought, exiting Rickover Hall and heading toward the dormitories at Bancroft Hall, *where the hell is Brent?*

The mid-afternoon sun was sharp and clear. As he walked, Tony replayed the past few weeks in his head. Brent had changed. He was quieter, distant, prone to vanishing for hours at a time. They'd been close since day one, closer than most brothers. Brent, an orphan, had latched onto Tony like a drowning man to a lifeline. At first, Tony hadn't known how to deal with it, but over time, their friendship had become effortless. Natural.

And if Brent was falling apart, Tony wasn't going to sit on the sidelines and watch. *If Brent is screwing up, it's my job to kick him in the ass and set him straight,* Tony thought.

Reaching Bancroft Hall, he climbed the stairs to the second floor and made his way to Brent's room. He paused outside the door, raised his fist to knock, then changed his mind. He turned the knob and pushed the door open.

What he saw made him stop cold.

The room was a disaster. An overturned chair lay on its side. Books were scattered across the floor. A drawer was open and halfway off its tracks. At other colleges, it might have been normal. Here, it was unacceptable.

Brent's roommates had both washed out at midterm, and as the top cadet, Brent had been granted permission to use the room solo. He'd removed the bunk beds and converted the space into a study. Now, it looked like someone had tossed a grenade into it.

Tony stepped carefully through the mess, made his way to the window, and yanked the shade. Sunlight flooded the room, and a groan rose from the bed behind him.

A lump shifted under the covers.

Tony turned, his mouth tightening into a frown. "Brent?"

No response. Just another muffled groan.

Tony took a step closer, then stopped when he saw the bottle on the nightstand. He picked it up slowly, dreading what he might find. The label read OxyContin. But what caught his eye was the name: Timothy Hughes.

Tony's eyes narrowed. Hughes had been one of Brent's former roommates, the one who dropped out.

"Goddammit, Brent," Tony muttered. With one motion, he yanked the covers off the bed.

Brent flinched, curling tighter into a ball and shielding his eyes from the sunlight.

"What the hell are you thinking?" Tony barked. "You think you can handle this stuff?"

"Close the blinds," Brent groaned. "You're killing me."

Tony ignored him. "Get up." He reached down and grabbed Brent's arm, hauling him off the bed.

Brent screamed and twisted away, clutching his side. "Let go, you son of a—" He collapsed back onto the mattress, breathing hard, face contorted in pain.

Tony backed off, shaken. For a second, neither of them spoke. Then Tony's eyes fell again on the pill bottle. His blood boiled.

Brent, still grimacing, reached for it. He fumbled with the cap and shook out two pills.

Tony stepped forward and slapped them out of his hand. The pills flew across the room and bounced off the far wall.

Brent's head snapped up. "What the hell's your problem?"

"My problem? You're the one skipping class, hiding in your room, and popping pills prescribed to someone else!"

Brent sneered. "Look, Mother, I don't need a lecture. I've got this under control."

"Yeah?" Tony folded his arms. "Because this" he gestured to the wrecked room, the stolen meds, the dark circles under Brent's eyes "this looks real under control."

They stared each other down for several long seconds. Then Brent wordlessly picked up the bottle, popped two more pills, and slowly chewed them, never breaking eye contact.

Tony didn't move. But a new thought chilled him. *What if it wasn't just pills?*

"Is it just the Oxy?" he asked quietly.

Brent looked confused. "What do you mean?"

Tony didn't answer. He stepped forward, grabbed Brent's arm, and pulled up the pajama sleeve.

Brent cried out in pain again, but Tony didn't stop until he saw the bruise. A massive, deep bruise ran up Brent's forearm and disappeared beneath the sleeve. No needle marks. But the swelling, the discoloration, it was bad.

Tony's expression shifted. "Where did you get that?"

Brent pulled his arm away, wincing. "Relax. It's not what you think."

Tony didn't relax. His eyes traced the bruise peeking from Brent's shirt collar. "Is that one worse?"

Brent gave a half-laugh. "Much." He unbuttoned his pajama top and pulled it open.

Tony inhaled sharply.

Brent's chest and abdomen were mottled with ugly bruises, purple, blue, yellowing around the edges. The sight knocked the anger out of him.

"Jesus," Tony said. "What the hell happened to you?"

Brent leaned his head back against the wall. "It was an accident. I didn't want to deal with medical. The pills were all I had."

"What kind of accident?"

Brent hesitated. Then: "I got tackled by someone in body armor."

Tony blinked. "What?"

Brent didn't elaborate.

Tony stared at him, realizing that whatever had happened, Brent wasn't ready to share it. Not yet. "You sure you're alright?"

Brent gave a pained smile. "Right now, I feel like I got run over by a truck. But I'll be back in the game tomorrow."

Tony wasn't convinced. "I was out of line," he admitted. "I shouldn't have jumped to conclusions. I was just concerned because it seems like you've changed over the last few weeks. That's all."

Brent shrugged. "You were just worried. It's fine." But his smile was thin. His eyes drifted for a moment before refocusing. "Things have just been stressful," he added, almost under his breath.

Tony nodded slowly, lowered the blinds, and walked to the door. "Get some rest. I'll see you tomorrow."

The door clicked shut behind him. Brent stared at it for a long time. Then he swung his legs back into bed and pulled the covers over his head.

CHAPTER 8

"Good morning," called Tony as he spotted Brent approaching from the far side of the courtyard. Brent gave a small, tired wave and quietly fell into step beside him. They passed the weathered Tecumseh statue and stepped onto the well-worn red bricks of Stribling Walk, which stretched like a ceremonial carpet through Radford Terrace. The morning sun filtered through the thick branches of the old oaks overhead, casting shifting patterns of shadow and light across the path.

"How are you feeling this morning?" Tony asked, turning slightly to catch a better look at his friend.

"Sore. Really, really sore," Brent admitted, rolling his shoulders and wincing. His gait was stiff, like every step took effort.

Tony gave a faint smile. "Well, at least you sound more like yourself today. What's your afternoon look like? I was thinking we could go over the Systems Engineering assignment together. Maybe knock it out before the weekend."

"Sorry, Tony. I can't. I'm already behind in two other classes. I was planning to spend the afternoon in the library, trying to catch up on research. Want to join me?"

Tony shook his head. "Nah, I'll wait outside. One of those benches near the front gets great sun this time of day. I'll go over my notes and soak it in for a bit. I'll catch up with you after you're done."

He gave Brent a friendly pat on the back, only to see Brent flinch slightly. "Sorry, man. Forgot for a second."

Brent gave him a half-smirk and jabbed him in the shoulder with mock irritation. "See you later, Tony."

Brent turned and strolled toward the towering structure of Nimitz Library, named for Fleet Admiral Chester W. Nimitz. The angular lines of the building contrasted sharply with the historic charm of the Academy's older architecture. Tony watched his friend disappear through the doors before making his way to a red-painted bench nearby. He dropped his bag of books with a thump and sat down, stretching out his legs and tilting his face toward the sun.

He pulled out his Systems Engineering textbook, its spine already creased from overuse, and flipped through to the section they were currently covering in class. Blocking out the passing footsteps of midshipmen and the occasional chirp of birds overhead, Tony focused in on the dense, diagram-heavy pages.

Hours passed unnoticed. Tony finally closed the third textbook and rubbed his tired eyes. The sun had shifted, casting longer shadows across the square. He leaned back, groaned, and stretched until his joints cracked. As he gathered his books, a loud bang from the direction of the library caught his attention. He turned quickly, scanning the area. One of the doors had been slammed open, and a student stumbled out, doubling over and vomiting into the neatly trimmed bushes that lined the entrance.

Just another plebe suffering the aftermath of a rough night, Tony thought. Still, something about the way the guy moved seemed familiar. He squinted and leaned forward.

Wait. That's Brent.

Tony's heart dropped. His bag hit the ground as he rushed toward him.

"Hey! Are you OK?" Tony shouted, reaching Brent's side in seconds.

Brent was hunched over, one hand on the concrete planter, his body heaving. "Leave me alone. I'm fine," Brent croaked without looking up. He shrugged Tony's hand away and tried to stand, but he staggered sideways.

Tony stepped in front of him and placed both hands on his shoulders to steady him. What he saw made his stomach tighten.

Brent's eyes were bloodshot to the point of bleeding. The tiny veins had ruptured, filling the whites with deep red streaks. Sweat poured down his pale face, soaking his collar and dripping onto the sun-warmed sidewalk. His right pant leg was torn, and below the fabric, his knee was scraped raw and oozing blood.

Tony's voice was tight with concern. "Who did this to you? Are they still in the library? Should I call security?"

Brent straightened just enough to speak. "Help me sit down," he whispered, his voice trembling.

Tony wrapped an arm around his back and steadied him as they slowly shuffled to a nearby bench. Tony could feel the icy chill in Brent's hands, despite the heat of the day. Once seated, Brent slumped against the bench and closed his eyes.

"Do you know who it was?" Tony asked, trying to keep his voice calm.

Brent let out a shaky, bitter chuckle and rubbed his face with both hands. "Yeah. I got a good look. Five-nine. Dark hair. Wearing camo with Russian insignias."

Tony blinked. "Wait. You're saying there's a Russian soldier in the library?"

Brent shook his head. "No. I think I heard someone say it was Mission Bay. Near San Diego."

Tony's concern morphed into frustration. "Damn it, Brent! I'm trying to help, but I can't do that if you won't give me a straight answer. What actually happened? No more dodging."

Brent's laugh was hollow. "You want the truth? The truth is... I think I'm going insane. That's what you're thinking, right?"

Tony exhaled slowly. "I'm your friend. Just talk to me. Whatever it is, I'll listen."

Brent stared hard at him, searching his face. *Fine. Let's see how you handle this.*

"I was in Mission Bay. I got hit in the face with the butt of an AK-47 while trying to stop a Russian from executing a Navy SEAL. The SEAL had been shot, couldn't move. I saw the Russian raise his rifle to finish him off. I jumped him. Took him by surprise, but he recovered fast. Threw me off, knocked me senseless. Last thing I saw was the SEAL getting the upper hand—choking the guy out, knife in hand..."

Tony stood up and slung his bag over one shoulder, his face a mask of disbelief.

"Where are you going?" Brent asked.

Tony looked down at him, eyes filled with frustration. "When you're ready to tell the truth, let me know. But don't waste my time with crap stories."

He turned and walked away, leaving Brent alone on the bench, breathing hard in the afternoon sun.

CHAPTER 9

Tony's phone alarm began to beep softly at 5:30 a.m. on Saturday, rousing him from a light sleep. With a practiced hand, he silenced it, careful not to wake his roommates. He slipped out of bed, pulled on a worn T-shirt and a pair of shorts, then slung his running shoes over his shoulder by the laces. Moving with the quiet discipline ingrained in all midshipmen, he padded into the hallway in his socks, the cool floor a slight shock to his feet. Most of the cadets were still deep in sleep, taking advantage of the weekend. Normally, Tony would've done the same, but not today.

Yesterday's conversation with Brent was still churning in his mind, and Tony needed clarity. Running always helped him find it. When his thoughts tangled, his legs took over. With each mile, the clutter in his head faded, leaving only the rhythm of breath and motion.

Outside Bancroft Hall, the massive dormitory that housed generations of Naval Academy midshipmen, the morning was still and quiet. He sat on the steps and slid his feet into his shoes. The familiar creak of worn leather and the soft swish of tightening laces grounded him in routine. As he stood and shifted his weight to settle into the shoes, a subtle release flowed through his shoulders. The sun was just beginning to rise, casting soft light over the campus.

Tony began at a slow, deliberate pace, crossing the courtyard and turning left onto Cooper Road. The breeze coming off the Severn River carried the scent of brine and damp grass. He passed the soccer fields, picking up speed. His strides grew longer, stronger. He had loved running since high school, where morning runs were his sanctuary. Growing up in a noisy household with four siblings, he had found his peace in the solitude of those early miles.

When he arrived at the Academy, one of the first things he'd done was scout out routes. He had three-mile and six-mile loops, and a challenging ten-mile circuit that carried him over the Naval Academy Bridge, past the marina, and down to the Sailing Foundation. There, he could watch cadets unfurl sails and glide silently across the water, catching the wind like wings.

Today, he chose his favorite six-mile route. It would take him along the river, across College Creek, and past the Naval Academy Cemetery. The path was quiet, save for the occasional chirp of waking birds and the rhythm of his shoes on pavement.

Leaving the soccer fields behind, the first rays of sunlight painted golden lines on the Severn. When he passed Nimitz Library, he instinctively slowed. That was where everything had gone sideways with Brent yesterday. The memory stung, but he shook it off and focused on the wooden walkway ahead. The bridge over College Creek was lit with soft pools of light from the overhead lamps, still active before dawn. His shoes struck the planks with a sharp cadence, the sound bouncing off the still water. The evenly spaced posts of the guardrails blurred beside him, like silent sentinels marking his path.

By the time he finished his loop later, those lights would be off. Their artificial glow would give way to daylight.

Approaching the cemetery, Tony instinctively slowed to a walk. It wasn't fatigue that slowed his pace; he hadn't even broken a sweat yet. This part of the run always gave him pause. The rows of white and gray headstones stood as reminders of sacrifice, of the cost of service. No matter what weighed on him, this place always helped him see things more clearly.

He stepped off the path and gazed at the field of markers, letting the silence settle over him. It had become a ritual. No matter the chaos in his life, the solemn quiet of this place brought him back to center.

His thoughts turned to Brent. Brent had been his best friend since their first year. Their bond had surprised Tony at first. Both were strong-willed, decisive, and unafraid to lead. Tony had expected rivalry. Instead, they had become brothers. Their personalities didn't clash; they complemented one another.

Tony had always seen himself as the kind of leader who charged into battle. He made quick decisions and acted decisively. Brent, on the other hand, saw the battlefield from above. Where Tony would rally the troops and take the hill, Brent would study the terrain, the enemy, and every angle before committing. Tony was the captain on the bridge during combat. Brent was the admiral in the war room, thinking three moves ahead.

And Brent wasn't just smart. He was brilliant. Nearly a genius, in Tony's view. He had a deep love for his country, a strong sense of duty, and the discipline to back it all up. That's how he earned a full scholarship and rose to the top of their class. He had done all that without parents, without wealth, without connections. Just grit and intellect.

Tony slowed to a complete stop, struck by a sudden thought so strong it nearly tripped him up.

Brent doesn't lie. It was more than trust. It was a truth Tony felt in his bones. Brent wasn't capable of deception, not even to save himself. Lying was antithetical to everything Brent stood for.

That realization lifted something heavy from Tony's shoulders. The tension that had coiled in his chest all night seemed to unwind. He took a deep breath, exhaled slowly, and smiled.

His gaze swept the headstones once more, and he offered a silent thanks to those buried here. Their presence had once again given him clarity.

Snapping to attention, Tony raised his hand in a crisp salute. Then he turned, his decision made. Breaking into a run, he retraced his path at full stride. He flew across the wooden walkway, the air cool against his skin. He knew exactly what he had to do next.

It was time to call the senator who had nominated him to the Academy. He had a favor to ask.

CHAPTER 10

Two days later, Brent was lying on his bed with a damp washrag draped over his eyes when he heard a soft knock at the door.

"Come in," he called.

Tony opened the door and stepped into the room. He walked over and stood beside the bed, concern evident in his expression. "How are you feeling?" he asked.

Brent sat up slowly and tossed the washrag toward the foot of the bed. His gaze met Tony's with a flicker of suspicion. He hadn't seen Tony since the scene at the library.

"Better. I can't shake this headache, but it's manageable."

Tony nodded and reached into the bag slung over his shoulder. He pulled out a small stack of papers and dropped them onto Brent's blanket.

"What's this?" Brent asked, flipping through the pages.

"It's a report about a Navy SEAL team that raided a Russian stronghold at the University of California," Tony said as he took a seat in the chair across from the bed. "They rescued two professors who'd been taken hostage. The mission was a success, aside from one SEAL taking a bullet to the leg."

Brent stared at the pages. Realization slowly dawned on his face. "You believe me," he said, voice rising with surprise. He winced and rubbed his temples. "You believe I was really there. This proves I wasn't making it up."

"Not exactly," Tony replied, leaning back in the chair.

Brent's hopeful smile began to fade. "I don't understand. The injury matches exactly what I told you."

"The problem," Tony said, pressing his fingertips together, "is that the mission happened two days before you collapsed outside the library."

Brent blinked. "That... that can't be right," he muttered, standing up and beginning to pace the small room. "That doesn't make sense."

Tony watched him carefully. "You could've seen the report ahead of time and made the story fit. With those pills you've been taking, maybe you convinced yourself it was real."

Brent stopped pacing and turned to face him. "I swear, Tony, it's not like that. I only took those pills when I absolutely had to. You have to believe me."

"I do," Tony said, his voice quiet but steady.

Brent froze. "Wait. You do? Really?"

"Yeah. And I'm still trying to figure out what that means."

Tony stood and walked over to the window. The early morning sun was beginning to chase away the shadows along Radford Terrace. Outside, squirrels darted across the grass, paying little attention to the cadets walking to and from Bancroft Hall. Tony leaned against the window frame and glanced back toward Brent.

"I had to pull some serious strings to get that report," he said, nodding at the papers. "Information on classified missions doesn't just get passed around. There's no way you had access to that—especially not the medical report or mission debrief."

Brent dropped back onto the bed with a sigh of relief. "Thank you, Tony. I can't tell you how much that means. But hang on," he said, frowning. "You believe me just because I couldn't have had the report? That's a big leap. You really think I was in California two days ago?"

Tony reached for the stack of papers and flipped through them until he found the page he was looking for.

"Here's a section from Captain Lasseter's mission debrief," Tony said, reading aloud. "'One round hit me in the leg and I went down hard. As I lay there, a Russian soldier approached and raised his rifle. I thought it was over until someone tackled him from behind. They hit the ground hard, but the Russian recovered fast. He broke free and smashed his rifle butt into the other guy's head. While he was distracted, I managed to lunge up, get my arm around his neck, and stab him in the kidney with my K-BAR. I remember the dead weight dragging me down. I must've blacked out, because the next thing I remember was Lt. Miller wrapping a bandage around my leg. The lieutenant wanted to search for the guy who saved me, but we had to move. I hope he made it. Damnedest thing, though. I could've sworn he was wearing a Naval Academy midshipman's uniform. Must've been the blood loss messing with my head.'"

Tony looked up from the page and met Brent's eyes. "I don't have all the answers. But there's too much here to ignore. So I'm listening."

Brent took a deep breath and sat upright. "I don't know where to start. I feel pulled toward certain objects—like a magnetic force I can't resist. The closer I get, the more it feels like something... radiating. Fear, maybe. When I touch the object, I'm hit with this overwhelming surge of emotion. I black out. When I wake up, I'm wherever the person in danger is. It doesn't make sense, but it keeps happening."

Tony stood again and began pacing slowly. He tapped a finger against his lips as he thought. "Some psychics claim objects can hold emotional energy, especially during traumatic events. I've never believed in that stuff... but this?"

Brent looked up. "Tony, how did I get to Mission Bay? That's nearly 3,000 miles away."

Tony stopped pacing. "That's hard to explain. But what gets me even more is that you arrived two days before you ever left."

Brent's expression paled. "Do you think that's what's making me sick?"

Tony sat beside him. "It's too much of a coincidence to ignore. Maybe whatever's causing this... this transport, or whatever it is, takes a huge toll on your body. Maybe you're not actually sick, just completely drained."

Brent ran a hand through his hair. When he pulled it away, several strands clung to his fingers. He held his hand up, eyes wide. "I don't think so."

Tony saw the loose hair and went still. Neither of them said a word, but the silence said everything.

CHAPTER 11

Helen reached up with her free hand and adjusted the helmet of her radiation suit, trying to find a position that didn't dig into the bridge of her nose. She had been working in the reactor room for over three hours, carefully interfacing the submarine's stealth system with the nuclear reactor's fuel assembly. Her most recent task, installing the final segment of piping, had just been completed. Now she needed to verify that none of the new components interfered with the insertion of the control rods—a critical step.

A muffled voice broke through the hum of the reactor room. "Ms. Sinclair? Are you ready to insert the control rods?"

She turned and saw Jake, the sub's nuclear power plant technician, peering at her through the face shield of his helmet. At first, Jake had been reluctant to let her touch anything without personally inspecting it himself. But after the first hour of working together, he realized that, compared to her knowledge of the reactor system, he was barely qualified to carry her toolbox. She didn't just understand the technology, she could have designed it.

Sweat stung her eyes, sliding down from her hairline and collecting inside the collar of her suit. Even with the reactor shut down, the uranium fuel continued its slow decay, generating heat. A specialized cooling system pumped chilled air into the room, but it was barely enough. The radiation suits, sealed tight for safety, trapped the heat, turning the work into a grueling physical ordeal.

"Yes, let's cycle the control rods up and down a few times to verify clearances," she said. "Jake, you monitor pipes one and two. I'll keep an eye on three and four. Then we'll switch positions and double-check."

Jake gave a nod and moved to the opposite side of the fuel assembly, taking his position.

Helen waited until he was ready, then tapped the button on her wrist to activate the suit's built-in wireless intercom. It connected directly to the nuclear reactor control room.

"Control, this is Sinclair. We're ready to test the control rods. Bring them down slowly."

The reply came through her helmet speakers, slightly distorted but clear enough. "Copy that, Ma'am. Lowering control rods in five... four... three... two... one... lowering now."

Inside the reactor, the rods began their slow descent.

Uranium-235, the fuel source for the Trumpetfish's reactor, was inherently unstable. When struck by a neutron, each atom split in a process called nuclear fission, releasing a large burst of energy and additional neutrons. These secondary neutrons collided with other uranium atoms, triggering a chain reaction that could escalate quickly. This process generated the energy that powered the submarine, but if left unchecked, the reaction could intensify too rapidly, resulting in a nuclear runaway... a meltdown.

To control the reaction, the Trumpetfish's reactor used long rods made of hafnium, a gray metal chemically similar to zirconium, known for its ability to absorb neutrons. Encased in aluminum cladding, these control rods interrupted the chain reaction by capturing the free neutrons. Adjusting their position allowed precise control over the reactor's energy output. It was imperative that the newly installed piping did not obstruct the rods' motion. Even the slightest interference could render the control system inoperable.

Helen crouched slightly, eyes fixed on the slow descent of control rods three and four. They glided past the piping she had installed, clearing the equipment with ample space. Nothing was even close to obstructing their path.

She turned her head and saw Jake watching his side. When their eyes met, he flashed a grin and held up both thumbs.

Helen smiled inside her helmet. It was a small thing, but it felt like the culmination of years of effort. For so long, her stealth system had been theory, models, and simulations. Now it was becoming real, fully integrated with one of the most advanced propulsion systems on Earth. She took a long, steadying breath. Her vision was coming to life.

CHAPTER 12

"I'm going with you next time," Tony stated matter-of-factly as he plopped down in a library chair across the table from Brent.

Brent stared at Tony. "What do you mean you're going with me next time?"

"The next time you transport, I'm going with you. I've thought about it, and it's the only way to prove what's going on."

Brent regarded him thoughtfully, then slowly set his pen on his notebook and closed his textbook. "How would that be possible?" he asked after a moment. "I don't control when it happens. It just... happens."

"I've been thinking about that. You told me that right before you transfer, your vision gets a slight blue tint."

"Yeah, like looking through blue sunglasses. So?"

"Have you ever arrived without your clothes?"

Brent blinked in surprise. "Of course not!"

"Exactly. Your clothes aren't part of you, but they make the trip. So I think there's a kind of aura or energy field around you before it happens. I think it wraps around whatever you're in contact with."

Brent considered it. "You think it would wrap around you too, if you're touching me?"

"If I'm in contact with you, why not?" Tony's confidence faltered slightly as he said it out loud. It sounded even more ridiculous than it had in his head. Then again, believing Brent could actually teleport through space and time hadn't sounded especially sane either. And yet here they were. He had been looking for a way to prove Brent's story was real, not just a hallucination brought on by stress or medication. This idea... joining Brent, was the only way to know for certain.

"Well," Brent said, "I appreciate what you're trying to do. But this thing is making me sick... really sick. I can't let you risk going through that."

"Fine," Tony said quickly, standing up. He had expected that answer. "Then let's head over to medical. Get checked out. Let them run some tests, see if you're stable. Maybe talk to someone about the hallucinations. They'll write you a prescription and clear this whole thing up."

Brent's chair scraped loudly as he shoved it back. He crossed his arms tightly across his chest. "You know damn well if I tell them this story, my Navy career is over. They'll think I've lost it. I'll be lucky if they don't lock me in a padded room."

Tony crossed his arms and leaned back in his chair, meeting Brent's stare. They sat like that for a long, silent moment, each challenging the other.

Finally, Brent sighed and looked up at the ceiling. "Maybe I am crazy. Maybe I should go to medical."

Tony leaned forward, planting his palms on the table. "If you really think you might be crazy, then let's find out together. Let me go with you."

Brent narrowed his eyes. "You set me up for that."

Tony grinned. "Strategic thinking. I am ranked near the top of the Academy in tactical warfare."

Brent shook his head, but a smile crept across his face. "You bastard."

Tony stood. "So when do we leave? Do you wave your hands and chant something? I'd really prefer some kind of spellcasting. You know, for dramatic flair."

Brent smirked. "Sorry to disappoint. No hand-waving. I told you, I get drawn to objects. When it happens, it happens."

"All right. Boring, but workable. Let's go looking. Maybe something will trigger it."

For the next two hours, they wandered the library. Brent moved slowly, trailing his hand across rows of books, pausing occasionally when something caught his attention. Tony stayed close, lightly resting a hand on Brent's shoulder, pretending to steady himself while secretly hoping physical contact would bring him along.

"I give up," Brent said as they exited the library. He walked down the steps and shook his head. "Nothing's happening."

Tony stopped him. "Let's try somewhere else. How about the Academy Museum?"

Brent considered it. "I haven't been there in forever. Sure. Maybe we'll get lucky."

They made their way across campus toward Preble Hall, which housed the United States Naval Museum. The building was nearly empty at this hour, and their footsteps echoed across the foyer's polished pink marble floor.

Inside, they moved through the exhibits. Tony found it difficult to stay focused on Brent. The museum always stirred something in him: pride, humility, a deep sense of gratitude. Seeing the faces and belongings of men and women who had served reminded him why he wore the uniform.

He let go of Brent's shoulder and wandered to a nearby display. "Hey, Brent, check this out," he called over his shoulder. "It's a video on the Battle of Leyte Gulf. I wrote a paper on this. One of the biggest naval battles ever. First time the Japanese used kamikazes."

When Brent didn't answer, Tony turned and saw him staring at a large floor display. It featured a twisted piece of metal from a deck gun.

Tony walked over. "This is new. From the USS Winston Churchill. That battle just happened a few months ago. I wouldn't want to have been there. That had to be terrifying. Right, Brent? That must've been as scary as—"

He stopped midsentence. Brent stood frozen in front of the display. His eyes were fixed on a shattered wristwatch positioned beside the mangled deck gun.

Tony stepped closer. "The torpedo must've hit right near this thing. Broke the guy's watch. He survived, though. Pretty wild. You see this, Brent?"

But Brent didn't answer. His hand was reaching toward the watch. His breathing turned shallow, and his eyes began to flutter.

Tony saw it then, a faint blue glow radiating off Brent's skin.

"Oh, hell," Tony whispered as he reached out with trembling fingers.

CHAPTER 13

Tony watched as his trembling fingers reached out toward Brent. The moment felt disconnected from reality, as though his hand belonged to someone else entirely. The air seemed thick, the world around him slowing to a crawl. Every movement was exaggerated and heavy. As his fingertips brushed the fabric of Brent's sleeve, a jolt of white-hot pain surged through his hand. The agony was immediate and overwhelming, flashing like a lightning bolt through his arm. A crushing pressure exploded in his skull, and suddenly his entire vision was consumed by a vivid blue glow.

The sensations that followed came in waves, each one more intense than the last. There was no pattern, no rhythm, only escalating torment. One second, he felt enveloped in blistering heat, as if submerged in molten light. The next, his skin seemed to freeze and crack, the cold so severe it felt like his flesh was being peeled from his bones. His eyes burned as if seared by heated metal rods. Colors he couldn't describe... mostly reds and yellows, smeared and flared in his mind like violent fireworks. He reached out blindly, desperate for something real, something to anchor him. But there was nothing. His thoughts fractured, scattered like leaves in a storm. Pain was the only constant.

Then, without warning, the glow vanished. The intensity faded. Tony blinked. His vision returned, blurry and dark. He was on his knees, palms flat against a wet, metallic surface. Before he could make sense of anything, his stomach convulsed, and a dry heave racked his body. His head felt thick, like it had been stuffed with cotton. His ears buzzed as if they were filled with static.

He forced himself to focus. It wasn't a floor… it was a deck. A ship's deck.

He staggered to his feet, only to have another surge of pain shoot through his skull. Bright sparks danced in his field of vision. He steadied himself against a nearby bulkhead and turned slowly, trying to understand where he was.

Then came the blast.

A thunderous explosion slammed into him, launching his body backward. He hit the deck hard, his ears ringing violently. Blinking through the pain, he looked out toward the sea beyond the railing. What he saw filled him with dread.

They were under attack.

All around him, ships roared through a raging sea. Cannons fired in rapid succession, each concussion sending geysers of seawater skyward. It pelted him like needles, soaking his skin and clothes until they clung to him like a second layer. He tasted salt on his lips, sharp and metallic.

His eyes stung, and he wiped his sleeve across his face, spotting blood from a bite to his lip. The sky, stained with a deep orange glow, was streaked with contrails from jet fighters that screamed overhead.

As he stood, the ship's deck rolled beneath his feet. He reached for the rail, gripping the cold, slick metal to steady himself. Before he could move again, a voice rang out to his left.

"Torpedo!"

The cry snapped him into action. He turned and saw Brent running full speed toward the forward deck, his boots slipping across the wet surface as he grabbed for the rail with one hand, shouting as he ran.

"Torpedo in the water!"

Tony's gaze followed Brent's. A sailor manned a mounted .50-caliber machine gun, locked into a harness, unaware of the threat. The crashing plumes of seawater and the roar of artillery masked Brent's voice. Tony sprinted to the rail and peered over the edge.

A V-shaped ripple cut through the water, speeding directly toward them—toward the gunner's position. And toward the ship they were on.

Tony didn't hesitate. He shoved away from the rail and ran full tilt after Brent. By the time he reached them, Brent had finally gotten the gunner's attention. The gunner unlatched his harness and leaped clear just as the torpedo struck.

The explosion hurled all three of them into the air. They tumbled like leaves in a storm, limbs flailing as they hurtled over the railing and into the sea.

Tony didn't remember hitting the water. When he opened his eyes, he was submerged. Panic threatened to take over. He kicked furiously, fighting his way to the surface. When he broke through, he gasped for air and choked on the smell of fuel mixed with salt.

Gagging and coughing, he whipped his head around. Flames danced across the waves, mingled with debris. The ship and the surrounding vessels had pulled away during the chaos, continuing the battle further out to sea. The roar of gunfire and explosions had diminished, now just distant echoes fading into the horizon.

"Brent! Brent! Where are you?" he yelled, swallowing more saltwater. He spit it out, bile rising in his throat.

A wave lifted him, and through the smoke and wreckage, he saw movement. Brent clung to a partially submerged piece of debris, his arm twisted through the straps of a flak jacket.

Tony swam toward them with frantic strokes. He reached the gunner first and pushed him up onto a floating section of wreckage. Then he turned to Brent.

"Brent!" he shouted, shaking his shoulder. Brent's eyes fluttered open. He looked around, disoriented.

"Where is he? I had him! He..."

"I've got him. He's right here. He's going to be fine," Tony assured him.

But when he looked at the gunner again, his stomach clenched. The man's face had gone pale gray.

"Damn it. He's not breathing!"

Tony hauled himself onto the wreckage and began CPR, tilting the gunner's head back and breathing into his mouth.

Brent tried to climb up to help, but the debris shifted dangerously.

"Stay in the water! You're stabilizing it!"

Tony focused on the CPR, pressing on the man's chest, breathing again, and again. Time felt frozen. Then, the gunner's body convulsed. He lurched forward and vomited seawater before collapsing again, this time with the faint rhythm of breathing.

"Is he... is he dead?" Brent whispered.

"No. Unconscious, but breathing," Tony panted, exhausted.

Brent exhaled and glanced toward the distance. "Tony... we were on a guided missile destroyer. That was the USS Winston Churchill."

Tony wiped stinging seawater from his eyes and squinted at the battered vessel. "Looks like she's still upright. Doesn't appear to be listing. She may have taken the hit and kept going."

"Uh, Tony?"

Tony turned and followed Brent's gaze. A shard of metal had impaled the gunner's leg. Blood swirled in the water around them.

"Hold him steady," Tony said as he tore the man's pant leg open and began wrapping the fabric around the injury. "This will help keep the metal from shifting. It's tight, but we have to stop the bleeding. We won't have light much longer."

Night settled in. The sea grew quiet. The sounds of battle faded. Only the creaking of the wreckage and the shallow breaths of the wounded man remained. Tony and Brent took turns sitting on the floating debris, pressed close to keep the gunner warm.

"You think someone will find us?" Brent asked.

"Eventually. Probably not until sunrise. It's too dark for a search now."

"Think he'll make it?"

Tony looked at the young man beside him. His skin was pale, but his breathing remained steady, if shallow.

"I don't know. He's in shock. We're barely holding on ourselves."

The night dragged on, silent and endless. They listened to the wounded man breathe, the two of them sharing the cold, heavy stillness. It was the longest night either of them could remember.

CHAPTER 14

Tony was in the water, taking his turn holding onto the wreckage, when the first light of dawn crept over the horizon. The outlines of the debris around them gradually sharpened, becoming clearer in the dim morning light. He looked over at Brent and the wounded gunner, both lying on what looked like the broken remains of a shattered shipping container. Brent had drifted off to sleep, his arm resting protectively near the gunner's chest. Reaching out, Tony placed his hand near the gunner's mouth and nose. A faint puff of air confirmed he was still breathing.

The transition from dawn to daylight was swift over open water. Soon, the sky was glowing bright, and the sea shimmered in the morning sun. Tony watched as Brent stirred, then sat up with a sudden jolt, his eyes darting around. When his gaze landed on Tony, his shoulders dropped, relief evident.

"Sorry, man. I didn't mean to crash like that," Brent said. "Give me a second, and I'll trade places with you."

"Nah, I'm good for now. We'll switch in a bit," Tony replied.

"You sure?"

Tony nodded, and Brent relaxed, immediately turning his attention to the injured sailor. "His name's Dawson," he said, examining the patch on the man's uniform. Brent leaned in, listening to the slow but steady rhythm of the gunner's heart. "It's weak, but holding."

He moved too fast as he sat back up, causing the debris to rock with the swell. Tony scanned the surrounding water. "There might be something useful nearby," he said and released the wreckage, kicking out into the water with a lazy dog paddle. He drifted from one floating object to another, inspecting each piece for anything helpful.

"Find anything?" Brent called after a few minutes.

Tony had latched onto a chunk of wood... possibly a broken table. He was just about to dismiss it when something on the crest of a wave caught his attention. A larger piece of debris bobbed in and out of view with each passing swell.

"Brent! I think there's someone over there!" Tony shouted, adrenaline overriding exhaustion as he pushed off and began swimming with all the energy he had left.

Brent squinted in the sunlight and spotted the object Tony was heading toward. "Tony! Wait! Hold up!" he called out. But Tony didn't hear. He was too focused, his mind racing with the possibility of another survivor.

When Tony reached the wreckage, his heart sank. A body lay draped over the flotsam, held in place by a life vest. The man's skin was charred, his uniform blackened and torn. The unmistakable stench of burned flesh hit Tony like a wave, and he recoiled, stomach churning. Fighting the rising nausea, he kicked backward, giving himself space to breathe.

After a moment, he composed himself and swam back to the body. Gritting his teeth, he slipped the life vest off the lifeless man. One side was scorched, but it still floated. Tony pulled it on and, taking long, slow strokes, made his way back to Brent.

He reached out to grab the container. "He's dead," he said quietly, his voice flat. Every word carried the weight of exhaustion and horror.

"I know," Brent replied softly. "I could see from here. I tried to stop you."

Brent slipped into the water and helped Tony up onto the floating debris. Tony removed the life vest and handed it to him before collapsing onto the wreckage. He pressed the heels of his hands into his eyes, as if trying to wipe away what he had just seen.

With the vest secured around his chest, Brent floated chin-deep in the water, staring off into the horizon. The other body still drifted near the wreckage Tony had left. Brent couldn't tell if the burning sensation on his cracked lips was from salt or something else entirely. Tears, maybe.

We weren't sent here to save him.

Time passed. Hours bled together. Tony slept on the wreckage while Brent faded in and out, one arm hooked through a split plank to keep from floating away. The ocean was calm, deceptively peaceful.

Then a low, rhythmic thumping echoed across the water.

Brent blinked, startled fully awake. Shielding his eyes from the harsh glare of the midday sun, he squinted upward.

A helicopter.

"Tony! Tony, wake up!"

Tony sat up quickly, confused at first. Brent pointed toward the sky. An MH-60S Sierra helicopter was bearing down on them, rotors slicing the air.

"They see us!" Brent shouted.

The chopper slowed, hovering above them. The downdraft churned the sea into chaos, spray hitting them from all directions. Tony leaned over the gunner's body to keep him from rolling off the debris.

A booming voice called through a loudspeaker. "Hold on! We're sending down the basket!"

A rescue basket descended slowly, swaying as it neared the surface. The rotor wash twisted it in circles. Tony reached up, missed once, then caught it. He guided it onto the container.

Saltwater stung his eyes as he struggled to maneuver Dawson into the basket. The wreckage bobbed violently with the added weight, but Tony secured the straps and held the basket steady. He looked up and gave a thumbs-up to the crew chief leaning out the side of the helicopter.

The winch engaged, and the basket began to rise, spinning gently as it lifted into the sky. Inside the cabin, a medic moved quickly, assessing Dawson's injuries as the basket was pulled in. Once the gunner was safely aboard and transferred to a stretcher, the crew chief readied the basket for another trip.

He pushed it out the door again, watching it descend toward the ocean. Then he paused. The surface below was empty. Just moments ago, there had been two men—one on the wreckage and another in the water. Now, both were gone.

CHAPTER 15

Tony and Brent stood at ease in a line with eight other midshipmen on a raised platform to the right of the lectern. Before them, the President of the United States addressed the entire assembled Academy. The honor of standing beside the Commander-in-Chief had been granted to the top ten firsties, a recognition of their academic and leadership achievements.

"For too long, the American people have tolerated a foreign army occupying our land." The President's voice rang out with power and clarity. He paused, sweeping his gaze over the crowd. Past the cameras and media, he focused on the hundreds of midshipmen who listened in silence. In their eyes, he saw a mix of emotions—excitement, anxiety, concern—but overriding them all was determination. These young men and women had entered the Naval Academy during wartime, and there were no quitters at Annapolis. His chest swelled with pride.

"For too long, we have tolerated our families and fellow citizens being held against their will. For too long, we have allowed the deaths of Americans to go unanswered. That is intolerable!"

His voice thundered through the public address system, each syllable charged with emotion. He gripped the lectern until his knuckles turned white. Another pause. The crowd was silent, hanging on his every word. Releasing his grip, he closed the leather binder of notes and leaned slightly forward.

"Some would say that America has been at war for eighteen long years. I respectfully disagree. I say America has been under attack for eighteen years. And for America, the war begins today."

A roar of applause erupted. The President's words had lit a fire. His message was clear: hope, purpose, and a return to the ideals that had once made America a beacon of freedom and strength. For this generation of future officers, his words carried the promise of renewal. They had grown up during a time of chaos and uncertainty. Their allies had distanced themselves, and their leaders had seemed overwhelmed. Now someone was standing up and declaring that it was time to fight back.

As the ceremony concluded, the President stepped away from the lectern and began shaking hands with the midshipmen on stage. When he reached Tony, Tony stood tall and offered his hand.

"It's a pleasure to meet you, Mr. President," Tony said.

"No, the pleasure is mine," the President replied with a warm smile. "It's young men like you who will help restore this nation's greatness. I understand the sacrifices and hard work it took for you to be standing here today. We need that strength and commitment now more than ever. Thank you—for your service and your dedication."

Tony grinned as the President moved on to Brent.

"I hear you're at the top of your class, young man," the President said, clasping Brent's hand.

"Yes, sir," Brent replied, his voice full of pride. Then he gave Tony a playful nudge with his elbow. "But my friend Tony here isn't making it easy. I expect him to overtake me any day."

The President glanced back at Tony with a glimmer of amusement. "Good. Competition reminds us there's always room to improve, always another level to reach."

He returned his attention to Brent. "But for now, you are the top midshipman, and I have a small token I'd like to give you."

He turned and took a small velvet box from an aide. Opening it, he revealed a gleaming medallion.

"This is the Distinguished Graduate award I received for my lifetime of service to the Navy, to the Academy, and to the nation. I imagine you've already earned several awards of your own, but I want you to have this one as a reminder. If you stay focused and keep making the right choices, there is no limit to what you can achieve."

Brent swallowed hard. "Yes, sir. It's a tremendous honor. I'll try to be worthy of it."

The President gave him a firm nod and placed a hand on his shoulder. "I have no doubt that you will." He shook Brent's hand again, then turned and waved to the crowd before heading toward the waiting motorcade.

As the President's entourage of black SUVs pulled away, Tony turned to Brent.

"Jeez, Brent! That's the most prestigious award at the Academy. I can't believe he gave you his Distinguished Graduate medallion."

Brent grinned as he looked down at the box in his hands. He studied the medal for a moment, then slowly closed the lid. A thoughtful expression passed across his face as his gaze followed the departing vehicles.

Tony noticed the change and asked, "What's wrong?"

Brent hesitated. "I don't know. It's probably nothing. It's just... when he shook my hand, I felt something."

Before he could explain further, a crowd of midshipmen surrounded them, clapping Brent on the back, congratulating him, and peppering him with questions about what the President had said. Whatever Brent had started to say was lost in the celebration.

CHAPTER 16

Later that day, deep within the White House's Situation Room, the President sat surrounded by the Joint Chiefs of Staff and senior members of the National Security Team. The room was dim, lit primarily by the glow of high-definition tactical displays mounted across the walls. All eyes were fixed on a central screen showing a map of the western Pacific Ocean. A tight formation of icons crept steadily away from the China Sea. These were not mere symbols; each represented a warship. Destroyers, cruisers, and carriers accompanied by a flood of metadata that hovered above them like ghostly labels. Ship classifications, weapons payloads, velocities, and projected routes glowed faintly in the ambient light.

Dashed lines stretched eastward across the Pacific, showing their anticipated trajectory. Right in the middle of their projected path, alone and unwavering, was a single blip marked USS Albuquerque. The notation identified it as a United States ballistic missile submarine one of the most powerful and secretive vessels in the Navy's arsenal.

"Well, sir," said Admiral Williamson, the Chief of Naval Operations, turning slightly toward the President, "you wanted to make sure they knew we were coming. I think it's safe to say that we now have their full and undivided attention."

The President didn't immediately respond. His eyes remained locked on the map. The room fell into a respectful silence. Then, without turning, he asked, "Any updates on the Russian submarine reported near the Alaskan coast?"

A secondary monitor flickered to life, switching to a map of Alaska. A single red dot pulsed roughly ten nautical miles off the coastline, hovering near the entrance to the Port of Nome.

Admiral Williamson stepped toward the screen and pointed. "Last contact was approximately four hours ago. It's moving slowly, and all indicators suggest it's heading toward Nome, most likely to take advantage of the port's sheltered position and existing missile defense coverage."

The President narrowed his eyes. "So let me get this straight. They send an entire carrier strike group bristling with anti-submarine weaponry straight toward our ballistic missile sub, and rather than pulling their own sub back to reduce tensions, they reposition it into a defensive stronghold."

"Yes, sir. That's our current analysis," Williamson replied. "They seem to be countering our show of strength with one of their own."

The President leaned forward slightly, folding his hands in front of him. His voice dropped into a quieter, more deliberate tone. "So they've chosen escalation. Interesting. And here I thought they might blink."

Another general, seated further down the table, muttered, "Looks like they're calling your bluff, Mr. President."

That earned the President's full attention. He turned toward the general slowly. "Bluff? No, General, this isn't a bluff. A bluff is a lie, a posture that hides your true weakness behind empty threats. What we're doing is different. This is a saber rattle. That means we're shaking the scabbard, letting the world know we have a blade and we're willing to use it, even if we haven't drawn it yet."

He turned his attention back to Admiral Williamson. "Tell the Albuquerque to disappear. I want her off the grid and submerged so deep not even the ocean remembers where she went."

Williamson gave a short, crisp nod. "Yes, sir. That's what she was built to do."

He and a few others began gathering up their briefing folders and tablets, preparing to leave.

The President leaned back in his chair and spoke again, this time more casually. "Going somewhere, gentlemen?"

The movement around the room stopped. Chairs that had begun to scrape back were quietly pushed forward again. Officers and advisors resumed their seats, casting uncertain glances at one another.

"We're not done," the President said. "We've been reacting for too long. Today, that ends. It's time to move beyond deterrence." The President paused and took a small, controlled sip of water before continuing. "If they've misread our intentions, and believe we were only bluffing, then we need to show them otherwise. It's time we stopped rattling our saber and drew the blade. Johnson, if you would."

Johnson, a civilian intelligence advisor seated at the operations console, tapped a few keys. The large screens in the room transitioned, flickering briefly before displaying high-resolution satellite imagery. Rows of Chinese and Russian aircraft sat clustered together on the tarmac of a sprawling airbase. The field was heavily fortified, with missile batteries stationed at key points along the perimeter.

Silence settled over the room as they absorbed the images. And then, without warning, General Timons the Air Force Chief of Staff stood abruptly. He walked to the screen, leaning in to scrutinize a row of parked aircraft.

"That's Fallon Air Base," he said, voice tight. He turned to face the President, his face bright with emotion. "Sir, if you authorize a strike to retake Fallon, I'll personally fly lead on the first sortie."

The President didn't smile, but there was approval in his eyes. The room had shifted. What had started as a defensive meeting had become something else entirely.

The United States had just made the decision to go on the offensive.

CHAPTER 17

Captain Tyler J. Morris stood atop the sail of the USS Trumpetfish, breathing in the briny sea air as the vessel cruised at five knots over a calm Atlantic swell. The ocean stretched out endlessly, a mirrored sheet of blue beneath a cloud-dappled sky. The rhythmic slap of water against the hull was almost soothing. Morris took a moment to appreciate the serenity. He knew it would not last.

The Trumpetfish, a cutting-edge Valkyrie-class attack submarine, was a marvel of naval engineering. Unlike earlier designs that handled sluggishly on the surface, this vessel remained stable even at slow speeds. Below his boots, the most advanced propulsion and stealth systems ever developed by the Navy waited patiently for his command. Today marked a pivotal step in proving those systems in real-world conditions.

Less than an hour earlier, Ms. Helen Sinclair had arrived in the control room with a calm expression and a simple nod. Her words had been brief but decisive: the new system was operational and ready for sea trials. Her confidence matched her reputation. Morris had trusted her work from the start, but hearing it confirmed brought a thrill of anticipation.

This mission was classified at the highest level. Top Secret Presidential. That meant only a select few individuals even knew about the existence of the system they were about to test. Every person who did had been hand-selected by the President himself. There would be no second chances, no margin for error, and certainly no public record.

Morris had already brought the Trumpetfish to the surface and sent a short, encrypted message to COMSUBLANT—Commander, Submarine Forces Atlantic— informing them they were ready to proceed. The response came back in under five minutes: "Proceed at your discretion. Good luck."

Without hesitation, he had relayed orders to the crew to prepare for submergence. The entire ship had shifted into a state of focused urgency. Hatches were dogged, equipment was secured, and compartments checked with silent precision. It was time.

Turning away from the Atlantic breeze, Morris climbed back down into the sail and descended into the pressure hull, securing the hatch above him. The clang of the hatch sealing was a sound he knew well. Before they could test the new system, the Trumpetfish needed to do what it was built for: vanish beneath the surface of the sea.

Inside the command center, the change in atmosphere was palpable. The quiet hum of electronics mixed with the calm voices of officers confirming status reports. The room was bathed in a low red light, enhancing visibility at sea while minimizing their detection signature.

"Prepare the ship to dive," Morris said, his voice even but resolute. It carried the quiet strength of a man who had led sailors into the unknown before.

"Captain, all personnel are on board and hatches are confirmed sealed," replied Lieutenant Harris, the Officer of the Deck.

Morris nodded. "Then let's get to work."

"Yes, sir," Harris replied, turning toward the front of the room. "All ahead standard."

"Diving Officer, take her down," Morris ordered, the edge of command now fully present in his tone. The room snapped into motion.

"Aye, sir," came the response from the Diving Officer, who leaned over his Human-Machine Interface console. His fingers tapped out a precise sequence across the touchscreen, commanding the Trumpetfish's ballast tanks to flood. A quiet hiss echoed through the control room as seawater surged into the tanks, offsetting the sub's natural buoyancy.

The ship began to descend.

"Planesman, bring us to a fifteen-degree down angle."

"Aye, sir," the young sailor at the helm replied without hesitation. He adjusted the virtual controls with smooth, practiced hands, settling into his seat to monitor the angle.

The Diving Officer glanced toward Morris and gave a short nod. Morris returned it, a silent exchange of mutual respect between seasoned submariners at the beginning of a mission that could reshape naval warfare.

Morris shifted his stance slightly, trying to feel the descent through his boots. As always on the Trumpetfish, the movement was too smooth to detect with the body alone. Instead, he relied on the readouts and the instincts honed through decades of command.

He looked around at the streamlined banks of touchscreen consoles and updated displays. Gone were the analog dials and clunky switches of older classes. The Valkyrie-class was sleek, efficient, and dangerously quiet.

"Take her to two hundred feet. Make turns for twenty knots," Morris instructed.

"Aye, Captain," replied the Officer of the Deck. Orders were relayed with crisp efficiency.

Morris moved to the HLSD—the Horizontal Large Screen Display—that dominated the central bulkhead. A blinking icon marked the Trumpetfish's current position just off the eastern seaboard. With a few gestures, he zoomed out the map, revealing a broad stretch of Atlantic Ocean.

A dashed navigation line snaked along the coast, hugging the continental shelf while avoiding commercial shipping routes and known underwater hazards. Their path had been carefully plotted to maximize stealth while bringing them close to the operation's key test area.

He tapped the destination marker. The display shifted to a detailed bathymetric map filled with depth gradients, current vectors, and temperature markers. His eyes locked onto a feature labeled in bold letters: *Blake Escarpment.*

It was a massive underwater cliff, rising sharply from the ocean floor like a submerged wall. The area around it was known for strange current patterns and acoustic shadows—a perfect place to vanish.

This would be their proving ground. If Sinclair's system worked as promised, no vessel on Earth would be able to track the Trumpetfish.

Morris took a steady breath and folded his arms across his chest. "OK, everyone. Stay sharp and focused. The next few days may end up in the history books. Let's make sure we live up to the expectations."

CHAPTER 18

The Blake Escarpment is one of the most dramatic underwater features off the southeastern coast of the United States. Located approximately four hundred kilometers east of Florida, this massive, submerged cliff marks the abrupt edge of the Blake Plateau. Stretching more than six hundred kilometers in a north-south direction, the escarpment represents a sheer geological drop-off. The plateau itself lies at a depth of about five hundred meters, but the escarpment plunges nearly ten times farther—down to a staggering five thousand meters. It is one of the steepest and deepest oceanic cliffs in the Atlantic, a feature both feared and respected by those who navigate the depths.

To put the depth in perspective, the deepest recorded dive by a military submarine was achieved by the Soviet K-278 Komsomolets, which descended to around 1300 meters thanks to its titanium hull. In contrast, the USS Trumpetfish, part of the cutting-edge Valkyrie-class, had an estimated crush depth of two thousand meters. However, that number was theoretical. No one had ever pushed a Valkyrie-class sub to its limits in real-world sea trials.

Captain Tyler J. Morris stood at the HLSD—the large horizontal display that projected a real-time, three-dimensional map of the surrounding seabed. He watched intently as the rugged contours of the Blake Plateau unfolded across the screen. The Trumpetfish's advanced sonar systems continuously updated the display, feeding back high-resolution data as the submarine cruised silently at a depth of two hundred meters and a speed of twenty knots.

His eyes tracked the coordinates shown at the top corner of the interface. With a thoughtful glance at the screen, he gave his next order. "Reduce speed to ten knots and adjust heading fifteen degrees to port. Let's ease over toward the escarpment and hold position when we arrive."

"Aye, Captain," replied the navigator. He ran a quick calculation and added, "At that heading and speed, we'll reach the escarpment in approximately twenty minutes."

"Excellent. Lieutenant Harris, contact Ms. Sinclair and let her know we'll be in position shortly."

The Officer of the Deck stepped over to a communications panel mounted near the bulkhead and picked up the secure phone line. With practiced precision, he dialed into the Reactor Control Room.

"Turner here," came the voice on the other end.

"Jake, let Ms. Sinclair know we're on approach. We'll be arriving at the escarpment in about twenty minutes."

"Will do, sir." Jake hung up the phone and turned to see Helen Sinclair already watching him.

"Is it go time?" she asked with a smirk. Her eyes lit up with excitement as he responded by holding his thumb and forefinger close together.

"Lieutenant Harris says we'll be over the test site in twenty."

Her smile faded slightly as she nodded and turned toward the newly installed control stations that lined the room. A full suite of status displays pulsed quietly in green indicating the system was at nominal conditions.

She took a breath and released it slowly. "Well, Jake, the system says it's ready for action. We've got twenty minutes to kill. What do you think, a round of checkers? Or maybe catch an episode of that ridiculous reality show you love?"

He grinned. "Run another diagnostic?"

"Exactly!" she replied, eyes twinkling.

⁂

"Captain, we've reached the edge of the Blake Escarpment," Lieutenant Harris announced, reading from the position data displayed on his terminal.

"Very good. Move us directly above the escarpment and initiate a controlled descent to three hundred meters."

"Aye, sir." Harris turned to the helmsman. "Ahead slow. Bring us down to three hundred meters."

The Trumpetfish glided forward, easing off the plateau's edge and beginning its descent into the yawning darkness of the Atlantic. From this point, the cliffside plunged thousands of meters into the ocean's abyssal plain. Their

113

descent would barely scratch the surface of the depths below, but it was a critical step.

Inside the command center, tension coiled through the crew like a taut cable. Officers watched their monitors closely as the submarine adjusted its depth. The dim red lighting cast long shadows on their focused faces.

"Depth three hundred meters, Captain," the Diving Officer confirmed. His voice was steady, but slightly higher in his nervous excitement.

Captain Morris nodded and sat upright. "All stop."

"All stop," Harris echoed.

The Trumpetfish came to a gentle halt in the water, hovering silently in the blackness. At this depth, sunlight was nearly nonexistent. The area was part of what oceanographers called the Twilight Zone—a realm of darkness where visibility was limited and the pressure immense.

Suspended just above the near-vertical face of the escarpment, the submarine seemed to dissolve into the inky void. Its matte-black hull made it nearly invisible. They were alone here, far from shipping lanes, far from any prying eyes.

This is where it would begin.

The crew knew it. The Captain knew it. The Trumpetfish was ready.

CHAPTER 19

"Helen, are you ready?" the Captain asked over the communications system.

"Green lights across the board, Captain. We're ready," she replied, her voice carrying a note of excitement. It sounded slightly tinny as the system relayed her words from the reactor control room.

The Captain reached over and tapped an icon on his screen, switching the channel from the reactor room to shipwide broadcast so he could address the crew.

"This is the Captain," he said, his voice calm and commanding.

Throughout the submarine, everyone paused. Conversations ceased, and heads turned toward the speakers as the Captain's voice resonated through the compartments.

"We will be testing the stealth system over the next several minutes. You all know the importance of this mission. If this test succeeds, our submarine crews will no longer need to fear making the slightest noise while our enemies drop sonar buoys and depth charges to find us. A successful test today will mark the beginning of a new era in submarine warfare."

He hesitated for a second before ending the broadcast, just long enough to feel the gravity of the moment. In all his years at sea, few missions had carried stakes as high as this.

He tapped the icon again to end the broadcast and scanned the room. The crew members nearby stared at him with a mixture of tension and anticipation. He shifted in his chair, feeling the familiar weight of command settle across his shoulders.

All part of the job, he thought.

He tapped another icon to reconnect with the reactor control room. "Ms. Sinclair. Proceed with the test."

"Yes, sir," Helen's voice echoed from the overhead speaker.

He leaned back in his chair and took a sip of his coffee. It was cold, but he didn't notice. His mind was focused on what came next.

Helen's fingers moved smoothly across the display panels. Her hands moved with the calm confidence of someone who had rehearsed this procedure hundreds of times. Every action she took now had been practiced, simulated, perfected. But even so, there was an undercurrent of tension beneath the surface. This was the real thing.

"Initiating control modules now," she said, pressing the flashing icon. On the screen, indicators shifted from pale yellow to a vivid blue as the modules activated.

"Control modules online. Starting irradiation process now," she continued, aware the open comm line would transmit everything to the bridge.

"Irradiation commencing."

She glanced up through the reactor's thick glass window, watching as the control rods slowly rose to allow the nuclear reaction to intensify.

"System normal, Captain. Preparing to engage the stealth system."

She turned to Jake, seated at the adjacent panel and monitoring the reactor's core systems.

"Ready, Jake?"

"Green board," he replied without looking up. "Ready when you are."

Helen looked back at the primary display. All component indicators were normal. A small square labeled "Initiate Stealth Mode" pulsed softly.

"Initiating stealth system now," she said, pressing the square.

Suddenly, the display screens flickered, and the submarine gave a slight jolt—like a hiccup. For a moment, everything blurred. Helen blinked rapidly and swiped at her eyes, trying to clear the double vision. A bright warning flashed on her control screen.

"Reactor output just spiked... thirty percent!" Jake shouted. His voice was clipped with urgency as his fingers danced across his screen, switching views and pressing commands. "Adjusting control rods to stabilize!"

Helen grunted in acknowledgment; her focus locked on the cascading alerts. Her hands moved swiftly across the panel, silencing warnings and working to reset a circuit that had tripped during the power surge.

Jake's fingers moved with frantic precision, but sweat was collecting under his collar, stinging his eyes. Every second that passed meant a greater chance of losing control.

"What the hell is going on?" the Captain's voice thundered from the speakers.

"The reactor's output spiked, Captain. We're making adjustments," Jake called out, still locked in on his efforts.

"Captain!" the sonarman called. His station was just forward of the command chair. "I'm detecting something at the edge of our sensor range!"

The Captain leaned over and studied the screen. A single blip flickered at the edge of the display. "What the hell is it?" he demanded.

"Unknown, sir. I can't get a solid lock. It's too far out... and now it's gone." The sonarman's fingers danced across the touchscreen, navigating menus and pushing the sensors to full sensitivity.

"Damn it," the Captain muttered. He pulled his personal sonar display toward him and checked the data. He didn't like it. They'd chosen this location specifically for its remoteness. A phantom contact out here made his gut twist.

"Ms. Sinclair," he said, speaking clearly for the intercom, "we may have company. Shut the system down. We need to maneuver."

"Captain, we almost have it stabilized. We've adjusted the Ununoctium flow through the reactor and we can..."

"Shut it down, Ms. Sinclair. Now!" The irritation in his voice was sharp, his patience gone.

"Yes, sir! Shutting down, sir... sorry, sir."

Then, without warning, an explosion ripped through the submarine.

The force threw the Captain from his chair, slamming his head into the corner of the large horizontal display unit. Dazed, he fought to stay conscious as emergency lights flickered on and alarms began to wail. Shadows shifted in the red glow.

Then everything went dark.

When he opened his eyes again, Lieutenant Harris was crouched beside him, pressing a cloth against his forehead.

"Be still, Captain. You took a bad hit. You're bleeding."

"Report!" the Captain growled, wincing as pain lanced through his skull. His vision was doubled, and his stomach churned.

"There was an explosion aft. We've sealed off two sections to control the flooding."

"Torpedo?" He rubbed his eyes roughly, trying to focus. *A torpedo made sense. It fit. But no one had seen it coming.* That fact unsettled the Captain more than the explosion itself.

"Unknown, sir. Sonar didn't detect anything inbound. The blast took out propulsion, navigation, and primary communications. We're running on battery backup now." Harris exhaled slowly. "We're dead in the water, sir."

"Son of a bitch," the Captain muttered, trying and failing to stand. His balance was gone and the room spun wildly.

With effort, Harris helped him back into the command seat. The Captain sagged against the backrest, breathing hard.

"Sit still, sir. I think you've got a serious concussion. You need medical…"

"I've got the most classified system in the world on this sub… and its designer," the Captain snapped, gripping Harris's arm. "Something was hovering just outside our sensor range and now we've been hit!"

He slapped the intercom switch. "Jake," he called, then winced as pain surged through his head. "Report!"

"Jake here, sir. It's bad. The reactor tripped or tried to, anyway. When the explosion hit, we lost control. The emergency shutdown attempted to drive the rods into the core to stop the reactor, but they jammed. I'm trying to insert them manually, but no luck so far. If I can't shut it down…"

The lights flickered again, casting long shadows that danced across the reactor room walls like ghosts. Jake's voice trembled with exhaustion and something else… fear.

"Jake," the Captain cut in, his voice harsh. "We've got a threat out there. I need systems back online. I need power and I need it now!"

"Yes… sir. I'll do what I can."

The Captain leaned forward, gripping his console hard. He felt like he was shouting into the void, each command being debated… being denied. Every second without power was another second they were vulnerable.

"Jake, I don't care what it takes. Get the reactor under control and bring it back online."

"Sir, the contamination isolation system's engaged. That means radiation breach. Even if I can stabilize it… bringing it back online could be dangerous."

"Just do it!" the Captain roared, slamming the comm switch off. Nausea overtook him and he vomited over the arm of his chair.

"Captain!" Harris rushed to his side again, worry etched across his face. "We've got to get you to your stateroom. Let the medic take a look."

Morris stared up at him, blinking against the blur. His eyes couldn't focus. He saw multiple images of Harris, overlapping and twisting.

"Belay that," he rasped. "We've got work to do."

He opened a new comm line. "Torpedo room. I want Tubes One and Four loaded. Now."

"But Captain," Lieutenant Harris grabbed his arm. "we're dead in the water. If there's an enemy out there, we can't engage. We need to surface."

The Captain jerked his arm free. His pulse pounded in his ears, and a wave of dizziness nearly buckled him again, but he fought it off. He had to stay in control, had to stay the Captain, even if his body was screaming to shut down.

"Damn it, man! They're after the stealth system. It's our duty to deny them, even if it costs us our lives. This isn't about us. It's about national security."

Harris looked into the Captain's eyes. They were bloodshot and unfocused. "Sir, I know this looks bad, but the Trumpetfish is crippled. Even if we wanted to fight, I don't think we could."

"I don't give a damn what you think!" the Captain shouted. "You will follow my orders. Do you understand?"

"Sir, our guidance system is offline. We can't even provide targeting data to the torpedoes," Harris stammered.

He glanced at the flickering consoles and clenched his jaw. They weren't just blind, they were exposed. "And... respectfully, I don't think you're in any condition..."

"I want those tubes ready to fire!" the Captain cut in, his voice low but seething. "The moment we regain power, we'll fire blind if we have to. Do you read me, Lieutenant?"

"Yes, sir," Harris replied, his voice quiet. The fight had drained out of him.

Helen awoke slowly, her entire body aching. The control room was dark except for the faint glow of emergency lights above the doorway, casting shadows across the consoles.

A dull throb pulsed through her ribs, and her ears rang with the memory of the blast. Somewhere deeper inside, the worry had already begun gnawing at her. *Was it her system that failed?*

She realized she was sitting on the floor, slumped against the workstation where she had been overseeing the stealth system. As she tried to sit up, pain flared in her side.

She groaned softly and leaned back against the metal cabinet behind her, squeezing her eyes shut to fight off a wave of nausea. Her mind tried to replay the last few moments before the blast, but everything was fragmented into a mixture of sounds, alarms, the eerie flicker of warning lights. She must have blacked out again because when she opened her eyes, Jake was kneeling beside her, concern etched into his face.

"Easy, Miss Sinclair," he said, gently turning her head side to side. "Your color's better than it was. The blast threw you into the water shutoff valve. I think you cracked a rib. I called for a medic, but he's tied up with more serious injuries."

"What explosion?" Helen asked, her voice hoarse. Dread crept into her chest. She grabbed Jake's arms with trembling hands.

"Was it my system? Did I cause this?"

"No, ma'am. The Captain says it was another submarine. They must have hit us down near the missile storage room." He helped her into a chair.

"That's near the battery room." Her breath caught. "That's tied into the reactor system... How's the core?"

Jake hesitated. "It's out of control. The control rods jammed."

Helen turned sharply, pain flaring across her ribcage. The urgency overpowered the pain. She couldn't let this submarine become her legacy's grave. She wouldn't. "Then we need to go in there and free them."

"Hold on," Jake said. "There's more. We've got a radiation leak."

She froze. Cold fear washed through her. The words hung in the air like poison. Radiation leak. She had studied it, trained for it, even lectured others on the protocol. But in the pit of her stomach, a different kind of fear took hold. This wasn't a drill. This was survival.

She studied Jake's face, noticing the sheen of sweat on his brow. *The air is stifling... the cooling system must've failed.*

"Okay," she said finally. "We suit up, go into the reactor chamber, free the rods, shut it down, and then seal the leak. We'll stabilize the core and wait for help."

She started toward the radiation suit locker but stopped when Jake caught her arm.

"The explosion took out everything but the battery backups. Nav and propulsion are down. The only things still working are emergency lighting, limited comms, and a few other systems."

He hesitated.

"What is it, Jake? What aren't you telling me?"

"The Captain thinks the sub that hit us is coming back to finish the job. He wants me to bring the reactor back online."

Helen stared at him, horrified. "Back online? Has he lost his mind? Did you tell him about the leak? About the rods?"

"I told him. He... he didn't seem to care. He's in bad shape, but if he's right and we're about to be boarded... then we're sitting ducks."

"But if they were going to destroy us, they would've done it already," she said, trying to sound confident. Her voice betrayed her.

Jake didn't respond.

Helen looked at him, heart pounding. "You think they're here for the stealth system." The thought chilled her. Her name, her work, her signature embedded in every line of code. She had built the future—and someone wanted to steal it.

Jake nodded slowly. "Or worse. What if they want more than the system?"

Helen reacted as if he had smacked her in the face. The ramifications of a foreign power in possession of the stealth system were unimaginable. But the implications were there.

Their submarine was disabled but not destroyed. *What else could they want?*

"What do you mean?" Her voice was quiet.

Jake met her eyes. "What if they want its designer? What if they're after you?"

CHAPTER 20

Brent opened his eyes—and immediately wished he hadn't. The sunlight was so intense that even after he clamped them shut again, glowing orbs still burned behind his eyelids. Carefully, he cracked them open once more, squinting as his vision adjusted.

He was sitting on cold concrete beside a corrugated metal aircraft hangar. As he shifted, sharp cramps tore through his stomach, doubling him over and forcing him back to the ground. The pain was so intense that sweat trickled down his face, dripping onto his shirt. After a few agonizing minutes, the cramping eased enough for him to slowly lever himself up against the hangar wall.

He took in his surroundings, trying to get his bearings.

"Psst. Brent!" a voice whispered. "Over here."

Brent turned toward the sound and spotted Tony crouched behind a pair of weathered 50-gallon fuel drums stacked beside the adjacent hangar. Tony motioned urgently.

Keeping low, Brent ducked down and started moving across the twenty yards of open ground toward him. He only made it halfway before a deafening roar filled the air, stopping him in his tracks. He turned just in time to see an F/A-18 Hornet rip across the sky, its afterburners blazing like twin fireballs. A second and third jet followed closely behind, flying in tight formation as they vanished into the horizon.

Before Brent could react, a hand grabbed his arm and yanked him behind the fuel barrels.

"Are you stupid?" Tony hissed, his face just inches away. "You want us to get killed? Jeez, Brent."

Brent slumped back against the drums, breathless, and mumbled an apology.

Tony's gaze narrowed. "Do you even know where we are?"

"Uh... no, not exactly. Do you?"

Instead of answering, Tony jabbed a finger at the drum Brent was leaning against. Bold black letters were stenciled across the side: Fallon Air Station – Fallon, Nevada.

"Fallon?" Brent repeated, confused. "Why does that sound familiar?"

Tony gave him an incredulous look. "Come on, Brent. We're Navy. Top Gun? We watched it like twenty times last semester!"

Recognition hit Brent like a thunderclap. Fallon Air Station—home of the Navy's Strike Fighter Tactics Instructor program, still famously known as TOP GUN, as well as the SEALs' Combat Search and Rescue training facility.

But then his expression shifted.

"The Phoenix Alliance controls Fallon," he said slowly, a chill creeping into his voice. "They overran it years ago."

Tony nodded grimly. "We're behind enemy lines."

"Yeah, I know," Tony replied, peeking over the edge of the fuel barrels. "But something big is going on. I've seen at least twenty fighters circling the field—and look over there."

Brent followed his outstretched finger and spotted the smoldering wreckage of a Navy Viper helicopter embedded in a collapsed storage hangar. The tail rotor stuck awkwardly out through the roof, while the fuselage rested partially on the hangar floor, listing to one side. Smoke curled upward in thin, oily streams.

Crouching beside Tony, Brent watched as another fighter roared past the narrow gap between buildings, its jet wash stirring clouds of dust that whirled around them.

"Well," Brent muttered after a moment, "at least whatever battle just happened seems to be over."

Tony turned to him. "So what now? Do we just sit here and wait it out?"

"I don't know," Brent admitted. "Usually, when we land somewhere, all hell's breaking loose. But this time, it's quiet. No patrols nearby. No alarms. No gunfire." He stood and cautiously surveyed the airfield. "I say we check out that wrecked chopper. If the radios still work, we might be able to call for help."

Tony hesitated, then nodded. "Okay. Let's move—building to building."

The two darted between structures, sticking to shadows and keeping low until they reached the ruined hangar. They slipped through a partially buckled service door and immediately caught sight of the downed helicopter.

The Viper had apparently crashed through the roof, leaving a jagged hole in the hangar's ceiling. The bulk of the aircraft now lay on the hangar floor, its nose buried in a pile of twisted sheet metal. The tail boom extended upward at an awkward angle, still protruding through the damaged roof. Black smoke hissed from the twin engine nacelles.

"Wow," Brent breathed, running his hand along the scorched fuselage. "They must've lost both engines and crash-landed it right into the hangar."

"Pilot's dead," Tony said quietly, gazing into the shattered cockpit. The body was slumped forward in the seat, helmet cracked, face obscured by blood.

"What about the copilot?" Brent asked, stepping carefully over jagged shards of wreckage.

Tony shook his head. "Not in the seat. Looks like it was just the one guy."

"That's not right," Brent said, puzzled. "These birds always fly with two pilots. That's why they have tandem seating." He glanced down and spotted blood smeared across the five-point harness in the copilot's seat. Then he looked up at the open canopy.

"There's blood here too," he added. "Back here on the release lever. Did you open this?"

Tony, now fiddling with the cracked communications console, shook his head. "Nope. It was already open when we got here. I figured the crash forced it open."

Brent crouched beside the canopy frame. "No way. If the canopy popped during the crash, the handle wouldn't have blood on it. Someone opened this from the inside."

He looked back up. "Tony!"

Tony jumped at the sudden outburst. "Damn it, Brent! You trying to get us shot?"

"Sorry," Brent whispered, lowering his voice. "But I think the copilot made it out. There's blood on the harness and on the release handle. Someone unbuckled and ejected themselves—or climbed out."

Tony turned from the instrument panel, his expression shifting. "You really think he's still around?"

Brent nodded. "This is how it always works, right? We show up because someone needs help. This has to be why we're here."

Tony considered it, then looked at the bloody release handle. "Makes sense. Alright. I'll check the left side. You take the right."

He moved to step past Brent, but paused and grabbed his arm. "Be careful."

Brent gave him a smirk. "Thanks, Mom."

He hopped down from the wreckage and began moving along the right side of the hangar. The floor was a mess—overturned toolboxes, scorched maintenance gear, and broken racks filled with bent metal parts. Brent crouched low, careful not to step on anything that might echo through the cavernous space.

Then he froze.

"Tony," he called softly. "Did you hear that?"

"Hear what?" Tony whispered back, now only a few feet away.

Brent gestured toward the far corner of the hangar. "Sounded like something moved back there."

A low groan echoed faintly through the hangar, chilling the air around them.

Tony's spine stiffened. "Here we go."

They advanced slowly, moving past a row of metal storage racks loaded with aircraft components. At the far end, a dented pile of external fuel tanks leaned haphazardly against the wall.

As they rounded the final stack, they found the source of the sound.

A man lay curled up in the shadows, partially wedged between the tanks. Blood covered one side of his face, matted in his hair and dripping from a gash above his brow. He stirred again, a soft groan escaping as his body tried to rouse itself.

"He must've crawled in there to hide," Tony muttered. "But there's no way we're pulling him out through the gap he went in. We'll need to move one of these tanks."

Brent stepped to one end of the nearest fuel tank, wrapped his arms around the corroded metal, and heaved.

Nothing.

He let go, panting. "It's not budging."

Tony scanned the hangar until his eyes landed on the rafters above them. "Maybe we can use that," he said, pointing to an electric hoist mounted to a steel I-beam overhead. A frayed cable dangled uselessly from its hook.

Brent pressed a torn piece of his shirt against the pilot's head wound. "Yeah, good idea. We'll just need to find a sling."

Tony scanned the wall until he spotted a pegboard hung with lifting slings and chains. "Bingo," he said, already heading over.

He returned quickly, guiding the hoist's hook into place and threading a two-leg sling through the tank's lift points. After checking the tension, he looped the connector ring over the hook.

"Ready?" he asked.

"Go slow," Brent warned. "Just enough to see if the pile shifts."

Tony pressed the hoist control. The tank creaked, lifted an inch, and hung suspended.

Brent gave it a nudge. "It's moving. No weight resting on it. Go ahead and lift."

Tony raised the tank a few feet and carefully slid it sideways using the beam's trolley. Once clear, he lowered it gently to the floor.

He crouched beside Brent. "How bad is he?"

"The cut's messy, but the bleeding's slowing. He's been in and out. I think he's concussed," Brent said, checking the man's breathing. "He's also got bruising across his ribs. I wouldn't be surprised if a few are broken."

Tony let out a breath. "Honestly, I was expecting worse. I mean, last time we nearly got killed by a torpedo. This feels like a warm-up."

Brent grinned. "You're telling me. This is the first time that—"

A violent explosion cut him off.

The entire hangar shuddered as dust rained from above.

The blast rocked the hangar like a punch to the gut.

Both Brent and Tony dropped instinctively, shielding the injured man with their bodies as concrete dust and insulation rained down from the rafters. Another explosion followed, closer—this one shaking the walls hard enough to rattle the steel beams above them. Vibrations buzzed up through the floor.

"We've got to move!" Brent shouted.

They abandoned cover and sprinted to the hangar door. Brent shoved it open—and froze.

Thick, black smoke billowed skyward from several burning structures down the flight line. A row of Phoenix Alliance soldiers, weapons drawn, sprinted across the open ground just two hangars away.

Then came the sound of helicopter rotors.

Brent turned in time to see a chopper streak low across the runway. It was friendly—Navy markings on the tail—and it was in attack mode. The helicopter's nose tilted down, and a stream of 20mm cannon fire erupted, cutting a swath through the enemy ranks. Phoenix soldiers dove for cover as fire and debris exploded around them.

Before Brent could react, someone crashed into him from the side—knocking him and Tony both back into the hangar. The three tumbled to the ground just as a new explosion tore chunks of concrete from the wall, showering them with grit and debris.

The stranger rolled off them and sat up, brushing dust from his Navy flight suit. "Where the hell did you guys come from?" he demanded, eyes locking onto their academy uniforms.

"We... uh..." Brent stammered, searching for an answer.

Tony pointed behind them. "The copilot's still alive!"

The pilot's tone changed instantly. "Where?"

Tony led the way back to the injured man.

As soon as the pilot saw the motionless figure, he rushed forward and dropped to his knees beside him and performed a quick vitals check. Checking the pilot's name on his uniform he shouted, "Major Harris! Major, wake up Major! We've got to get you out of here."

"He's got a concussion," Tony said. "We think maybe broken ribs too, but he's breathing."

The pilot reached up and tapped his tactical comms earpiece. "This is Major Tom Little. I have one of the downed Viper pilots. He's injured and needs immediate medical assistance. I need an evacuation point." He held his hand over his ear so he could hear the response. A brief pause, then a static-laced response crackled through his earpiece. Little nodded. "Copy that."

He looked to Brent and Tony. "We've got a Blackhawk inbound, but we've got to move—now. They're inserting on the other side of the admin building. That's where I was inserted."

He hooked an arm under Harris's shoulders. "Grab his other side," he told Tony. "We've got to carry him. He's dead weight."

Tony moved into position, and the two lifted the injured pilot. Brent ran ahead, sweeping aside debris and clearing a path through the hangar.

They burst out into the smoke-choked air.

The fire was worse now with flames curled along the roofs of several hangars. The tarmac was littered with debris: burning panels, blown-out carts, twisted metal racks. They moved as fast as they could, weaving between the wreckage.

Brent shielded his face with his arms as they passed through a particularly hot patch of air. Just then, he glanced skyward... and his heart stopped.

Six Z-10 attack helicopters, sleek and angular, appeared over the eastern ridge. The Chinese gunships swooped in low, their stubby wings bristling with missiles.

"Tony! Hurry!" Brent shouted. He'd moved too far ahead.

He turned back and sprinted to rejoin the others, rounding the corner of a gutted maintenance building and nearly crashed into them.

"What are you waiting for?" he demanded, breathless. "Why aren't you getting on board the..."

He stopped.

There was no helicopter.

He turned to Major Little. "Where's the Blackhawk?"

Little gave him a grim smile and pointed east. "I had to call it in. She's been waiting behind a dune for my signal. Keep your eyes on the horizon and be ready. We won't have much time."

The words had barely left his mouth when the calvary arrived.

Two AH-64 Apache Longbows roared in from the east, 30 mm chain guns blazing. The Apaches charged straight into the fray, opening fire on the incoming Z-10s. The enemy helicopters scattered, breaking formation as tracer fire tore the sky. Dipping and weaving, the Apaches pushed the fight to the far end of the field.

Then the Blackhawk came.

It screamed in low, less than thirty feet above the ground. Rotor wash blasted the tarmac, kicking up huge contrails of dust and debris. It flared upward just before the LZ, dumping speed and rotating the aircraft to expose its side.

A crew chief manned the side door, seated behind a minigun. The massive, multi-barreled weapon was already spinning—ready to lay down thousands of rounds per minute. He held the gun trained toward the aerial battle, ready to join the fray if the Z-10s disengaged from the Apaches and headed their way.

The Blackhawk was still three feet off the ground when two crewmen with M-16s jumped out. As their jump boots touched the ground, they knelt down to maintain their balance against the rotor wash and scanned the area for hostile forces.

The pilot kept the rotors at full throttle, ready to send the helicopter skyward as soon as the passengers were aboard. The entire helicopter thrummed with the restrained power of the twin General Electric turboshaft engines.

Major Little and Tony hustled forward with Harris sagging between them. As they reached the door, a third crewman joined them and helped haul the injured pilot inside. He strapped Harris to a backboard with practiced precision.

Brent climbed in right behind them and secured himself in one of the fold-down seats. Major Little circled the helicopter and climbed into the co-pilot's seat.

The two men on the ground jumped in and positioned themselves in the doorway facing outward with their feet braced against the skids as the helicopter's pilot changed the pitch of the rotors and the Blackhawk vaulted into the air. Once in the air, the pilot spun the Blackhawk around and dipped its nose forward as it raced eastward away from the raging air battle behind them.

Outside the open doors, Brent saw a warzone unraveling. Apaches and Z-10s twisted through the sky in lethal combat, missiles flashing and gunfire streaking across the clouds of smoke.

"OK, guys," Major Little's voice came through the helicopter's intercom system. "Just what the hell are two midshipmen doing at Fallon?"

Silence.

He reached up and moved his helmet's mic closer to his mouth. He cupped his hand over the mic to block out some of the noise and called out to his crew chief, "Sammy, give the boys helmets with comm systems. I need to ask them some questions."

Once again, his only answer was the slight hissing of communication system. "Sammy? Can you hear me?"

"Yes, sir," came the crew chief's reply. His voice was uneven. "But... I can't, sir."

"What do you mean, you can't?" Little asked, his tone hardening.

"They're gone, sir."

Little whipped around and looked into the cabin.

Two empty seats.

"Damn it!" Major Little snapped. "You're telling me they got out before we lifted off?" He slammed his hand against the console, then turned to the pilot and tapped his shoulder. "Swing us around. We're going back. Get the Apaches on the comm. Let them know."

"Sir..." Sammy's voice cut in, hesitant and strained. "They didn't get out."

Little froze. "What do you mean, they didn't get out?"

"They're just... gone, sir. I was watching one of them and... and then he wasn't there anymore. They both vanished."

CHAPTER 21

Thomas barged past the President's secretary and shoved the door to the Oval Office open—only to be grabbed by two stunned Secret Service agents and slammed hard against the wall.

President James Conner looked up just in time to glimpse his Chief of Staff being hauled backward out of the doorway. A framed painting of the H.L. Hunley—the first submarine to sink an enemy ship—rattled against the wall from the commotion. The message was clear: his oldest friend had something urgent to say.

"It's okay, Johnson," the President called out, already returning his attention to the papers on his desk. "Let him in. I think he's learned the error of his ways."

A moment later, Thomas stepped through the doorway, straightening his tie and adjusting his suit coat. He offered a smirk as he slammed the door behind him in a very deliberate display of irritation.

"I take it this is important?" the President asked, setting his pen aside and clasping his hands together on the desk.

"James, we've taken Fallon," Thomas said, his voice surging with energy. He strode purposefully across the Presidential Seal inlaid in the floor, then jabbed a finger onto the desk's surface like a dagger. "We drove the bastards out. One runway is still operational, and we control the airspace over Nevada."

He peeled off his suit coat and tossed it over one of the sofas, then loosened his tie and popped the top button of his shirt. "We're doing it, James. We're beating the sons-of-bitches back. Damn, this feels good."

With a wide, boyish grin plastered across his face, he flopped down onto the nearest couch.

The President held his gaze and smiled. When he selected Fallon as the mission's objective, it wasn't just about recapturing a strategic airstrip. Fallon was a symbol—once the Navy's elite training base near Reno. The best aerial combat pilots in the world had come out of Fallon. Losing it had been a blow to the American psyche. Reclaiming it was a statement to the nation, to the Phoenix Alliance, and to the world: the tide was turning.

Fallon would now serve as a launchpad for air strikes into California. The U.S. wasn't just defending anymore. It was taking ground.

"How many casualties?" the President asked, rising from his chair and walking around the desk to take a seat on the sofa opposite his Chief of Staff.

"We lost one Viper pilot. His chopper went down—crashed into a hangar. But the copilot survived. Banged up pretty bad, but he's going to make it."

"That's it?" The President raised an eyebrow. "We took the base with only one casualty?"

"Caught them flat-footed," Thomas replied, reaching for the silver coffee tray an aide had left on the table. He poured two cups, handed one to the President, and took a sip of his own. "They had no idea it was coming."

He winced as the hot coffee burned his lip and let out a satisfied sigh. "Strangest thing, though—the Blackhawk crew that extracted the wounded pilot reported something... unusual. They claimed to have seen academy midshipmen on the ground."

He blew across his mug. "Probably just adrenaline messing with their heads."

The President said nothing, setting his cup down on the table. "Well, that should shake things up a little," he said with a smile, leaning into the armrest of the couch. "I bet General Timons is beside himself."

"Oh, he is," Thomas replied with a chuckle. "He was out on the runway, personally greeting every crew member as they returned. The whole operation was a decisive win—and the American people have waited a long damn time for one."

He leaned back, running a hand through his close-cropped hair. "I've been keyed up since the moment you authorized the strike. Now that it's done, I feel like I could sleep for a week." He grinned. "You should've heard the excitement in Timons' voice during the post-op briefing."

The President leaned forward. "Give me the full rundown."

Thomas set his mug down and launched into the briefing. "Last night, we sent a formation of Viper and Blackhawk helicopters across Death Valley, flying low to avoid detection. They landed just south of Las Vegas, on the shores of Lake Mead. Then, this morning, we launched three waves of fighter aircraft at Las Vegas as a feint, drawing the Phoenix fighters out of Fallon.

"Once the skies were clear, our helicopters moved in. They destroyed the remaining aircraft and engaged the ground troops. One Viper was hit by a shoulder-fired rocket—took out the engines and it crashed into a hangar. No explosion, thankfully. With the enemy pinned to one end of the airfield, we inserted a team to check for survivors."

He paused for another sip of coffee. "Like I said, one pilot was recovered with moderate injuries. The other didn't make it."

The President's face remained stoic as Thomas continued.

"While the rescue was underway, the enemy must've gotten a signal out—because six Chinese Z-10 helicopters showed up out of nowhere. But two Apaches were already in the area. They engaged immediately and gave the Blackhawk just enough cover to get our people out. Once the chopper was clear, the 82nd Airborne jumped in. From what I've heard, they swept the field clean and secured the runways without much trouble."

The President nodded. "What about our fighters over Vegas?"

"They flew to Fallon with enemy fighters breathing down their necks. But by the time the Phoenix aircraft got close, an additional wing of our fighters were already airborne from the newly captured base. I'd loved to have seen their faces—realizing too late that the planes rising to meet them weren't theirs. We shot down every last one of them."

The President stood and walked to the window overlooking the Rose Garden. Outside, the midday sun lit the blooms in a riot of color. But he didn't seem to notice. His gaze remained distant, contemplative.

Thomas joined him, and for a moment, neither man spoke. Then Thomas placed a firm hand on the President's shoulder.

"Well done, sir. Well done."

The President stared at the coffee cooling on the table. One battle won. A hundred more to come. "Call the Joint Chiefs..."

CHAPTER 22

President Conner strode into the Situation Room, smiling as he took his seat before the assembled Joint Chiefs of Staff and National Security Team.

"Well done, gentlemen. Extremely well done. We showed them the U.S. still has some teeth."

A round of applause broke out. The President caught more than a few voices exclaiming, "About damn time!" He let them enjoy the moment, then allowed his smile to fade.

"Okay. Now that we've reminded them what we're capable of—tell me how they're responding. Where's that Russian submarine?"

Admiral Williamson raised a hand, and the lights dimmed. Multiple screens flickered to life, displaying aerial imagery of Alaska's Port of Nome.

"This image was captured less than an hour before our strike on Fallon," the admiral said, pressing a button on a remote. The central image enlarged, focusing on a dark rectangular shape submerged just beneath the surface.

"The Stinger is clearly visible here, even though it's sitting in several feet of water."

He clicked again.

"This next image was taken less than thirty minutes after the attack."

The new screen displayed only a cloudy swirl where the sub had been.

"The vessel departed suddenly, with no attempt at stealth until it cleared the port. Then it vanished. We haven't detected it since."

"Thank you, Admiral. All right—what other response have they made?"

"Sir," said Secretary of Defense Tom Moreland, stepping forward, "we have reliable intelligence that a phone call took place between Russia's President Morozov and China's Supreme Leader Wei Cheng, their former Director General of International Affairs."

He pressed a button, and images of both leaders filled one of the monitors.

"Unfortunately, our source has limited detail on what was actually said, but it was reportedly a very heated exchange—each blaming the other's military for the failure at Fallon."

The image switched again—this time to video footage.

"This was taken at our National Guard base in Klamath Falls, Oregon—three hundred miles from Fallon. We have a special forces team embedded in the area. One of our Wasp drones, a hand-launched platform with a forty-five-minute flight window, captured this."

On screen, six large helicopters came into view.

"Those are twelve AMTSh-VN3s—the preferred aircraft for Spetsnaz insertions. Each one can carry up to twenty-five troops and is equipped with rocket pods, cannons, and air-to-air missiles."

The feed shifted to thermal imaging, giving the scene an eerie glow.

"As you can see, the engines were still hot when this was recorded," Moreland added. He turned to face the President. "It's our assessment that these six helicopters delivered between 100 and 150 Spetsnaz troops."

"Mr. President," General Brackson interrupted, leaning forward. "We have the 101st Airborne stationed at Warren Air Force Base in Wyoming. I recommend we deploy them to support the 82nd Airborne and stop any attempt to retake Fallon before it starts."

"I disagree," said General Timons. "Why risk American lives when we can take them out with air-to-surface missiles?"

President Conner leaned back in his chair, content for the moment to listen. The room filled with quiet, strategic debate as the Joint Chiefs weighed each course of action.

After several minutes, all eyes slowly turned toward the President.

"Obviously, we're not going to sit around and wait for them to mount a counterstrike. The fact they haven't launched missiles of their own suggests they want to retake Fallon, not destroy it. And with that Russian sub still unaccounted for—likely carrying nuclear warheads—now is not the time to escalate with cruise missiles."

He paused.

"Americans need something to rally around. Missiles don't inspire patriotic pride. Soldiers do. It's time to put a face on our victories. Let the American people see the finest fighting force in the world in action."

He looked directly at General Brackson.

"Send in the 101st."

CHAPTER 23

Scramming the reactor had failed.

Jake slammed his palm against the nuclear "kill" switch, expecting to hear the thud of control rods dropping into the core and see indicators flash as the reactor shut down. Nothing happened.

The rods hadn't moved. Not an inch.

The submarine's reactor relied on hydraulic pressure to hold the dense control rods suspended above the core. The kill switch was designed to dump that hydraulic pressure instantly, allowing the rods to fall, letting gravity and massive compression springs drive the rods into the core. Once in place, the rods would halt the nuclear chain reaction by absorbing the excess neutrons fueling it.

It was supposed to be foolproof. A fail-safe system designed to work even in the absence of electro/hydraulic power. The same principle was used in school buses: lose pressure, and springs automatically engage the brakes. Simple. Elegant. Effective.

Except this time, it didn't work.

Something was jamming the control rods.. whether mechanical obstruction, warped guide tubes, or debris lodged in the assemblies, Helen couldn't say yet. What should have been a gravity-assisted free fall into the core had come a dangerous standstill. Their only option now was to use hydraulic force to push the rods past whatever was blocking their descent and fully insert them into the core to shut down the reaction. That required hydraulic pressure, a lot of it... and they didn't have any.

The hydraulic system was in critical failure. Red indicators pulsed across the control interface as zone pressure faults, actuator response errors, and reservoir alarms flooded the screen, demanding immediate action. Diagnostic readouts confirmed the worst. Hydraulic lines had ruptured, pressure had collapsed to zero, and multiple subsystems had gone dark. Safety interlocks had triggered, isolating compromised sections, but the damage was already done. The entire system was unresponsive. Without pressure, the cylinders that drove the control rods couldn't move. The shutdown mechanism had been designed to protect the hydraulic system while relying on the fail-safe to insert the rods. But now, with the rods jammed halfway, they needed the hydraulic system back online—and they needed it now.

Inside the reactor room, Helen reached up to wipe the sweat stinging her eyes but her gloved hand knocked into the hood of her radiation suit. *Crap,* she thought irritably. *Third time I've tried that.* She shook her head, trying to fling the sweat away from her eyes. The air was stifling inside the suit, her breath fogging the face shield with every exhale.

She had been in here nearly an hour... sealed in a high-radiation environment, rerouting hydraulic lines, swapping out components, checking pressure gauges... and still the rods wouldn't budge.

"How are you doing, Helen?" Jake's voice crackled in her helmet.

She turned toward the thick glass of the reactor room window. Jake stood behind it, staring in with furrowed brows, his concern written across his face.

"I'm..." Her voice caught. Her throat was bone dry. She swallowed twice before forcing the words out. "I'm fine."

The hell I am. Her knees were weak, her vision blurred at the edges. But we don't have time for fine. If we don't get this reactor shut down soon, we're done. All of us.

She steadied herself and crossed the compartment to a row of hydraulic valves, scanning the pressure gauges. "I've rerouted another pressure line. We've got full pressure at the manifold's inlet. I'm checking the directional control valve that feeds the hydraulic cylinders on the rods."

She located the correct valve, DCV #12, and pulled a small Allen wrench from the toolbox. Reaching forward, she pressed the metal tool against the solenoid on the valve's left side.

Jake's voice came again. "Helen, what are you doing?"

"I'm checking the valve solenoids. That electrical spike may have fried them."

"Do you need a meter?" he asked, already half-turning to look for one.

"No need," Helen replied, eyes fixed on the valve. "If the solenoid is working, it'll create a magnetic field when energized. I can detect it with the wrench."

She traced the hydraulic lines with her eyes—steel tubes feeding the cylinders that moved the rods—and frowned. "Jake, I don't remember which side of this valve extends the cylinders. Let's check both."

"Copy that."

"Try energizing the left-side solenoid on DCV #12."

Jake tapped through warning-laden screens on the HMI panel. Red icons flashed across his interface assaulting his eyes. Finally, he found the right subsystem, located DCV #12, and pressed the icon for the left-side solenoid. It changed color, indicating an energized state.

Helen held the wrench steady. It twitched slightly—then tugged toward the solenoid. She let go, and the tool clung to the housing magnetically.

"This side is good," she confirmed, pulling it free. She moved to the opposite side of the valve. "Try the right-side solenoid."

Jake tapped the next icon.

"Come on, Jake," she muttered. "Anytime now."

"It's energized. Helen. The solenoid is showing green on the board."

She pressed the wrench firmly against the solenoid and let go. It fell straight to the floor with a clatter.

Helen allowed herself a grim smile. *Gotcha.*

"Jake, the right-side solenoid is toast. The power surge must have burned it out. I need to replace it. Shut the hydraulic pump off."

She watched the pressure gauge fall to zero, then unbolted the valve and removed the solenoid housing. Working quickly, she slid the fried solenoid free and grabbed a replacement from her toolbox. Her gloved hands made the work clumsy, but she managed to ease the new one into place and reattach the valve securely.

"Okay, Jake. Fire the pump back up. Let's see if this worked."

She gathered her tools while the pressure climbed on the gauge.

"Panel reads 2500 PSI," Jake confirmed from the control station.

"Finally," Helen replied, nearly whispering. Her legs wobbled, and she leaned against the wall. "Whenever you're ready."

"Energizing the cylinders... now." A harsh metallic screech tore through the room, then fell silent.

Movement flickered in the corner of her eye. She turned and saw it... the control rods were slowly descending into the core.

"Helen, it's working!" Jake shouted. "Get out of there!"

She didn't hesitate. She stumbled for the exit, muscles burning, slammed the hatch shut behind her, and collapsed against it, gasping for breath inside the thick suit.

"Reactor is under control," Jake said, voice sharp with urgency as he tapped the comms panel. "I'm bringing the system online at emergency power levels."

"Report!" the Captain's voice boomed through the overhead speaker.

"I'm restoring emergency levels now, Captain. You should see partial power coming online shortly. We had to replace multiple components and jury-rig a few connections. I recommend surfacing and evacuating nonessential..."

"Belay that! Give me as much power as you can!" the Captain snapped, cutting the comm abruptly.

Jake stared at the control panel for a beat, watching all the red icon still flashing in their urgency, and then turned to Helen.

She peeled off the radiation suit, her hair matted to her face, damp with heat and effort. As the suit crumpled to the floor, Jake's breath caught.

Her radiation badge, clipped to the front of her sweat-stained shirt, was black.

He stared at it, stunned. Helen slumped back against the bulkhead, too exhausted to react.

CHAPTER 24

Captain Morris shielded his eyes as the lights surged back on, flooding the room with a blinding intensity that stabbed through his skull. The sudden brightness triggered a fresh wave of nausea, and he doubled over, one hand gripping the side of his chair.

"Computers coming online, sir!" a voice called out, distant and hollow, like it was cutting through water.

Even with the lights restored, everything still felt smothered in fog. He blinked hard. Once. Twice. Nothing cleared. The haze clung to his vision, to his thoughts. His fingers dug into his temples as he tried to steady himself.

Screens flickered erratically across the command center. Crew members rushed from station to station, voices rising, hands trembling. The air was thick with static and confusion.

"Where's that damned sub?" Morris roared, his voice cracking under the pressure. The pain in his head surged. Hot, sharp, and splitting in its intensity. For a moment he thought his head might burst. He clenched the armrests and swallowed hard, forcing the bile back down his throat.

"Got him, sir!" the sonar tech called. "Two hundred yards off our port side and holding position. It's a Song-class. Chinese."

"Turn to port! Full power! Bring us around, damn it!" The Captain's voice was higher now—too high. There was a shrill edge to it, the kind of fear-laced urgency that made junior officers glance at each other in alarm.

Lieutenant Harris didn't hesitate. He lunged forward, hands locking onto the Captain's forearms, pinning them to the chair.

"Captain! We cannot do this!" Harris barked. "We're damaged and not combat-ready. We need to break contact and call for support." His grip tightened. "Please. That's a diesel-electric boat. There's no way they could have hit us from that range. The Trumpetfish has a hundred times their sensors, and we couldn't get a clean read. Something doesn't add up."

"Captain!" the sonar man interrupted again, his voice sharper now. "New contact! Small acoustic signature off our stern. It matches Navy SEAL underwater propulsion devices." A pause. "They're heading toward the forward hatch, sir."

The Captain surged to his feet, shoving Harris backward. The Lieutenant hit the deck hard, skidding across the floor.

Morris jabbed a trembling finger at him. "Are you satisfied now?" he snarled, then slammed the comm panel. "Major Hamlin! Get your SEALs to the stern hatch. We've got company!"

"Aye, sir," came the tight response.

Morris turned back, face flushed, eyes wild. "You're relieved of duty, Lieutenant! Get the hell out of my command center!"

Harris blinked, dazed. He sat there for a moment, stunned by the force of it all, then slowly climbed to his feet. All around him, young crew members stared wide-eyed and frozen. No one spoke. No one moved.

They're kids. Scared out of their minds. And he's going to get them all killed, Harris thought. *But there's nothing I can do.*

He smoothed his uniform shirt, stood at attention, and saluted.

Without another word, he stepped out of the command center and into the corridor. The moment he crossed the threshold, the Captain's voice roared from behind.

"FIRE!"

An icy chill ran down Harris's spine.

CHAPTER 25

Small canister lights recessed in the ceiling cast a dim, clinical glow onto the round mahogany conference table where three high-ranking generals sat in tense silence, their hands clasped tightly, knuckles pale. For two grueling hours, they had waited. These were not men accustomed to being summoned. They commanded armies, orchestrated wars, dictated terms of surrender. Yet here they were, ordered to abandon their field posts and report to this sealed, windowless room to await the Supreme Leader's presence. Not even a direct order; an aide had relayed the summons. A glorified messenger.

General Guntram Hargrave's jaw tightened. He slowly lifted his eyes and looked at the other two seated at the table. General Petrov and General Marko Shcherbatov sat hunched in quiet submission, avoiding eye contact like schoolboys caught cheating. *Disgraceful.*

"Bah," Hargrave muttered under his breath. He pushed back from the table with a sharp screech of wood on tile. The sudden sound snapped both men upright, alarm flaring in their eyes.

"General, what are you doing?" Petrov asked, his voice tight with confusion.

Hargrave rose, every inch of his frame radiating defiance. "What am I doing? I'm ending this charade." He looked down at them like they were fools. "The Supreme Leader didn't summon us. An aide told us to wait. A lowly aide." He gestured broadly. "And here we sit, like boys caught stealing a pie. Like beggars!"

He kicked his chair back under the table with enough force to jostle the surface. Water glasses trembled.

"No more. I've had enough of this farce." He snatched his officer's hat from the polished wood, placed it squarely on his head, and adjusted the brim with ritualistic precision. As he stormed toward the door, he paused, turning to face the others with a sneer that curled at the corner of his mouth.

"Auf Wiedersehen, gentlemen. I return to the field where soldiers still command respect. Give our illustrious leader my regards, assuming he ever graces you with his presence."

He executed a perfect military about-face and grabbed the doorknob. It didn't budge. His hand slipped, twisted again, but it remained locked. The sneer vanished. Confusion spread across his face, replaced quickly by anger.

"What is this?" he barked. He pounded his fist against the door. "Open up! Open this door immediately!"

A beat of silence.

Then the knob turned from the other side, and the door opened without a sound.

Standing in the doorway was Supreme Leader Wei Cheng.

"I hope I haven't kept you waiting, Herr General," he said, baring his yellowed teeth in something meant to resemble a smile. His voice was like glass dragged across concrete.

Hargrave's spine stiffened. The air seemed to grow colder.

Wei Cheng was dressed immaculately in a deep navy suit and golden silk tie, immaculate and calculated, every element chosen to radiate control. Without breaking eye contact, he stepped into the room, brushing past Hargrave like he wasn't there.

Petrov and Shcherbatov snapped to attention. Wei Cheng nodded slightly.

"General Petrov. General Shcherbatov." He didn't acknowledge Hargrave.

Hargrave returned to the table stiffly, muttering an apology, eyes fixed downward. *He wanted that,* Hargrave thought, his teeth grinding. *He wanted to humiliate one of us.*

Wei Cheng took his seat at the head of the table. He rested his elbows on the surface, fingertips lightly pressed together. He waited in silence until the others were seated. Then, slowly, he leaned back and placed both palms flat on the table. The overhead lights etched his features with harsh shadows.

"Now," he said, his voice barely above a whisper, "perhaps someone can explain to me how we lost control of Fallon Air Station."

He stood abruptly, voice rising in anger. "Twelve fighters. Six helicopters. One hundred and eight Russian soldiers. Gone. And what did we take from them?"

Spittle flew as he barked the answer himself. "One helicopter. You killed one pilot. ONE!" He slammed both fists against the table, causing several glasses to jump. "You allowed them to seize a runway. They're landing troops and supplies. Uncontested. On *our* soil."

He glared at each general in turn. None could meet his eyes.

"Do you have any idea what this means?"

A pause. Then his voice cracked with fury.

"It means you gave them hope."

General Petrov, still pale, cleared his throat. "Your Excellency, it is a temporary setback. Our special forces are already mobilizing. We will retake the airfield."

"You idiot!" Wei Cheng roared.

Petrov flinched like he'd been struck. His face drained of color. Wei Cheng inhaled deeply, held it, and slowly exhaled as he returned to his chair.

"You have no idea what you've done," he said, this time in a near whisper. "Hope... hope is contagious. It affects morale. It multiplies. You think this was just a battle? It was a message. One the American people heard loud and clear."

General Hargrave shifted uncomfortably in his seat. "With respect, sir, it was one engagement. The Americans can't believe it has any long-term meaning."

Wei Cheng turned his gaze on him with a stare so cold it stopped Hargrave mid-breath. The Supreme Leader's expression was unreadable. Calculating. Disappointed. As if his trusted dog had defecated on the floor.

He reached forward and retrieved a crystal tumbler from a silver tray. With deliberate slowness, he poured tepid water from a sweating pitcher. A single drip fell from the rim and struck the dark wood below with a soft tap.

Wei Cheng took a sip, then stared into the facets of the cut glass as if consulting something only he could see. With one finger, he traced a spiral in the condensation on the table.

"Once the seed of hope is planted, it can't be allowed to grow. It must be dug up. Root and all," he said.

He looked up, setting the glass down. "We must hit them hard. And we must do it now. Before the rot spreads. Suggestions?"

An eerie silence descended.

After several moments, General Shcherbatov stood. He began pacing with his hands clasped behind his back. His polished boots struck the floor with crisp military rhythm. Then, without warning, he stopped.

"We launch a nuclear warhead," he said. Calm. Cold. Certain. "From our Stinger submarine. A Bulava-class missile. One hundred fifty kilotons."

The air shifted. Even Wei Cheng appeared taken aback.

Shcherbatov smiled faintly. "It sends a message. A message they won't ignore."

Hargrave shot up from his seat. "That's madness!" he barked. "You want to give them a cause? A martyrdom? This will unite their people against us like nothing else ever could!"

"Wait." Wei Cheng raised a hand, stopping him mid-sentence. His voice dropped into something dark and reflective. "Maybe... maybe this is what we need. A reminder. Perhaps they've forgotten who we are. Forgotten the cost of arrogance."

Hargrave's voice rose with disbelief as he pointed an accusatory finger. "You worry about giving them hope and then propose another 9/11? You'll have every last American old enough to hold a rifle ready to die for that flag."

Wei Cheng stood, knocking his chair back. He swatted Hargrave's finger away with a sharp motion. "You forget yourself, General. I asked for options. Not idealism."

"Excuse me, Your Excellency," Petrov interjected, slowly rising. "But General Hargrave is right. A nuclear strike in response to one lost airfield will do more than unite their people. It will force their hand. The only reason they haven't responded in kind is restraint. That restraint will vanish the second we cross that line."

Wei Cheng turned slowly toward Petrov, eyes narrowing.

"Then tell me, General. What would you have us do?"

Petrov didn't flinch. His voice remained calm. "Kill one man."

Wei Cheng blinked, as if not sure he'd heard correctly. "One man?"

Petrov lifted a glass, tilting it toward the others in a mock toast. "The President of the United States."

Wei Cheng studied him for several seconds. Then his face broke into a slow, terrible smile. A rasping chuckle escaped his throat as he raised his own glass.

"Now that," he said, "is a strategy."

CHAPTER 26

B rent snapped the folder shut and lobbed it across the room with a lazy flick of his wrist. Reid yelped and caught it an inch from his face.

"Hey!" Reid exclaimed, stumbling slightly as he flopped down on the corner of Brent's bed. "You almost clocked me in the head!"

From the other side of the room, Tony lay sprawled across the arms of an armchair, one leg hanging off and an arm draped over his eyes. At Reid's outburst, he cracked one eye open. He caught sight of Brent's smug grin, then Reid's flustered expression, and gave a weary shake of his head before letting his eyes fall shut again.

Brent sauntered over and gave Reid a light, mock-patronizing pat on the cheek. "Relax, Plebe. If I had actually wanted to hit you, you'd still be on the floor."

Reid rolled his eyes but cracked a smile as Brent nodded toward the folder. "That's a solid report. You nailed the revision I suggested last week. Nicely done."

"Seriously?" Reid's eyes lit up. He tore the folder open and started scanning the pages like they might vanish.

"Seriously," Brent said, more sincerely this time. "You've been busting your ass on that paper, and it shows. You should be proud of it."

"Tony!" Reid shouted, kicking at the leg of Tony's chair. "He liked it. Brent actually liked it!"

Tony groaned theatrically and lifted a single finger, twirling it in the air in the universal sign for "whoop-de-doo."

Brent chuckled. "All right, Reid. Tony's half-dead and I'm not far behind. Take the win. Fix those few typos I marked and we'll go over it again tomorrow."

"Thanks, Brent." Reid stuffed the folder into his backpack and slung it over his shoulder. At the door, he turned and grinned. "Catch you guys after fourth period!"

Brent watched the door click shut. Then he eased himself back onto the bed, limbs heavy with exhaustion. He draped an arm over his eyes to block out the light and let out a soft groan as he tried to stretch the stiffness from his body.

Tony opened one eye again and studied him. "You good?"

Brent hesitated. "Yeah. I'm fine. You?"

Tony barked a humorless laugh. "I feel like crap. But I still think I'm doing better than you. Seriously, Brent, how do you feel?"

Brent sighed and closed his eyes. The aches flared beneath the surface like embers under ash. He pressed his fingertips to his temples, rubbing slow circles. "Honestly? Not great. I know something's wrong. I can feel it... deep down. It's not just exhaustion. It's like my body's running on the wrong frequency or something. Like there's a hum just beneath the surface that won't go away."

Tony sat up straighter, concern sharpening his features. "That's it. We're going. Emergency room. Now."

Brent peeled his arm from his face and looked at him with a faint, wry smile. "You and I both know they're not going to find anything. Whatever this is... it's not something a blood test or CT scan is going to catch."

"You don't know that!" Tony snapped, louder than he intended. He stood up, running a hand through his hair in frustration. "What if it's something treatable? What if it's just a vitamin deficiency, or some weird virus, or a misfiring nerve? You can't just lie here waiting for it to get worse."

Brent gave a low chuckle, his voice thin. "That's the thing, Tony. It already has."

Tony stared at him, heart pounding. He picked up a pillow and hurled it across the room. Brent batted it away, laughing weakly. The pillow ricocheted off the bookshelf, knocking loose a few paperbacks and a small velvet box.

Tony bent to retrieve the mess. The velvet box had sprung open slightly, revealing a folded ribbon. Curious, Tony lifted the lid. The President's Distinguished Graduate medal rested inside, its weighty metal catching the dim light.

He turned and held it up. "This... this was given to you by the President of the United States. Our Commander-in-Chief. You earned this, Brent. You didn't get this by luck. You got it because of your grit and brilliance and everything you've poured into your work and this country."

He crossed the room and placed the medal gently in Brent's hand. "Don't let whatever this is take all of that away without a fight. Even if the doctors can't fix it, you need to try. If not for you, then for everything you've already sacrificed."

Brent stared at the medal in his palm, the ribbon draping over his fingers like the weight of a decision yet to be made. Slowly, his expression shifted. Remorse, doubt, and something unspoken passed across his face.

A low hum filled Brent's ears. The world seemed to ripple. A faint, bluish shimmer danced around him for an instant.

Tony's eyes widened. "Brent?"

Brent swayed, eyes rolling back.

The velvet box slipped from Tony's fingers as he lunged forward, heart hammering.

CHAPTER 27

"**S**on? You alright?" Tony opened his eyes to find a gray-haired man bent over him, staring with concern. Easing his head back to work out a kink in his neck, he felt it contact something solid. Reaching behind him, he felt the rough surface of a concrete pillar. Looking to his left, he saw a long line of three-foot-tall concrete pillars separating the sidewalk from a grassy expanse.

"Son, can you hear me? Are you OK? Do you want me to call for an ambulance?" The man placed a hand on Tony's shoulder to get his attention.

"What?" Tony focused on the man and noticed a woman and two small children standing just behind him. "No, uh, I'm fine. I just... I was feeling a little sick to my stomach, but it's better now. Must've been something I ate," he lied, taking the man's offered hand and letting himself be pulled to his feet.

"Are you sure? You still look a little green."

"No, really, I'm fine." Tony glanced around, trying to spot Brent.

"Are you here for a visit, or are you stationed here?"

"What?" Tony turned back to the man. "What are you talking about?"

"Your shirt. I just figured you were here for a tour, or maybe assigned here as part of security."

Tony looked down at his Naval Academy T-shirt and absently tucked it in. "Tour of what?" he asked as he peered down the sidewalk, still searching for Brent.

Not hearing a response, he glanced back. The man was watching him with a perplexed expression. Then Tony noticed the little girl holding her mother's hand and pointing behind him with the other. Slowly, he turned around.

Across the grassy lawn sat the White House.

"Oh," he whispered to himself. "This is not good."

"Tony!"

He whipped around at the sound of his name and saw Brent gesturing to him from the shade of a large tree. Mumbling a quick thanks, he hurried over.

"Jeez, Brent. It's the White House!" Tony grabbed Brent's arm and jerked him closer. "Do you think we're here to help the President?"

Brent peered intently at Tony and gave a brief nod. "Yeah, who else? I was holding his achievement award. It's got to be him."

Tony stared back at him, then whipped his head around, scanning the area. "We've got to tell someone. Security or the Secret Service."

"They won't believe us, Tony," Brent said softly, his voice tinged with defeat. "What are we going to tell them? That the President is in danger, but we don't know when or how?"

"I know, but we've got to try. We can't take the chance of not telling them!" Tony grabbed Brent's shoulders and waited until Brent's eyes met his. "We could fail, Brent, and the President could die."

"I know, but... but they won't believe us. And then they'll arrest us. What if we disappear while we're in lockup? They'll have our names, Tony. They'll come get us and lock us up in some government research laboratory."

Tony released Brent and rubbed his eyes. Looking across the yard at the gleaming White House, he exhaled slowly. "We don't have a choice. He's our Commander-in-Chief. It's our duty to protect him—even if we end up in jail." Slumping against the tree beside Brent, he continued, "Look, we'll tell security about the threat. Believe us or not, they'll go on high alert. The President will be safe."

Brent closed his eyes and leaned his head back against the rough bark of the tree. He felt the dappled sunlight flicker across his closed eyelids as the wind stirred the branches above. Suddenly, his eyes popped open.

"Then we don't have much time!"

"Right! The Oval Office is down this way. There should be a guard station." Tony moved into a brisk walk along the sidewalk that followed West Executive Avenue, Brent close on his heels. Dodging clumps of tourists, they made their way forward. Several times, they offered apologies as they passed in front of people taking family photos with the White House in the background.

Breaking free into a clear area, Tony paused and looked around. "Look, there's the Rose Garden and that must be the Oval Office over to the left."

"Tony?"

He turned and followed Brent's gaze.

"You see that guy with the duffel bag?"

Tony scanned the sidewalk and spotted a small man in dirty denim jeans and a dark blue work shirt. He was rummaging through an old duffel bag lying on the ground in front of him. His hair was disheveled, and he had at least a week's growth of beard. Tony shrugged and turned back to Brent.

"Yeah, I see him. Looks like a bum. What about him?"

"His boots are polished."

Tony stared at Brent as the words sank in, then looked back toward the man and focused on his boots.

That's odd, he thought.

"I dunno. Maybe he's ex-military. Old habits die hard. So what?"

Brent started forward with a deliberate stride. "He's giving me a bad vibe. Come on."

Tony jogged a few steps and fell into stride beside him. "What are you going to do?" he whispered.

"I don't know yet. We'll think of something."

Suddenly, the man raised his head and stared at the two boys approaching. Slowly, he stood and called out to them.

"Hey... hey. You got a few bucks to spare? How about it, fellas? Just a few bills?" He stepped between them and his duffel bag, holding out a hand.

Brent made a show of patting his pockets, then shrugged. "Sorry. I don't have any cash on me. Tell you what... come with us and we'll get you a hot meal."

Tony watched as the man's eyes widened for a brief moment, then he grinned.

"No, no. Can't leave my spot. Someone else'll move in. This is a prime spot."

Brent gave a slow nod. "Well, have a good day." He started walking away, Tony at his side.

"Did you see his hands?" Brent hissed as they moved away.

"No," Tony replied, trying to picture them.

"His nails were clean and trimmed. His clothes were dirty, but he's the cleanest bum I've ever seen. I swear his breath smelled like mint."

Tony stopped and pretended to gaze at the White House. "What's he doing now?"

Brent turned and casually leaned against one of the concrete pillars. He looked over Tony's shoulder, back at the man.

"He's watching us."

Tony felt the skin on the back of his neck crawl. "Damn. You think this is the threat to the President?"

"Yeah. I think so," Brent replied softly.

Tony sighed as he glanced toward the Oval Office. "I think so too."

"Damn!" Brent shouted, then took off at a dead run toward the man.

Tony wheeled around just in time to see the man finish pulling an AT4 light anti-tank rocket launcher from the duffel bag and hoist it onto his shoulder. He dropped to one knee, aiming it toward the Oval Office.

Frozen in place by fear, Tony watched helplessly as Brent raced forward.

He's not going to make it in time!

CHAPTER 28

The President stood in the Oval Office, hands clasped behind his back as he gazed out over the South Lawn. The tree branches swayed in the breeze, casting shifting shadows across the cobblestone path that split the immaculately trimmed grass. On especially difficult days, he'd slip off his shoes and leave them behind on that very path—opting instead to walk barefoot through the lawn, grounding himself in the cool loam beneath his feet. It reminded him of simpler times: running barefoot as a boy through the woods outside his family's home in Burgess, Alabama. The memory always helped him find calm.

But not today.

He sighed and stepped away from the window. *No time for tiptoeing through the tulips,* he thought. The 101st had secured Fallon. Runways were operational, and reinforcements were already en route to prepare for the push toward Reno and Carson City. Soon, he and the Joint Chiefs would turn their attention to California. Since the liberation of Fallon, he'd braced for retaliation but so far, silence. And that silence was unsettling.

He perched on the edge of his desk and looked back out the window. In the distance, tourists ambled along the sidewalk beyond the South Lawn fence. He watched a young couple pass their phone to a stranger and pose for a picture. He smiled faintly. *If they zoomed in far enough,* he mused, *they'd spot me here, watching them from the Oval Office.*

Then, something caught his eye.

To the right, a man was sprinting down the sidewalk.

What in the world—

The door burst open with a deafening crack.

Secret Service agents surged into the room, barking commands. Before he could speak, they were on him— grabbing him, shielding him, hustling him backward toward the door to his private study. His shoes scraped against the floor as he stumbled to keep pace, barely registering the press of strong hands and the urgency in their eyes.

CHAPTER 29

Brent's legs churned and arms pumped as adrenaline surged through his body like a live wire. He tore across the lawn with a single, burning thought: the President was in danger, and it was his duty to stop the threat, no matter the cost. There was no hesitation, no fear, only instinct and training. The possibility that he might die didn't even register. He had already made peace with that years ago.

He could still remember that quiet night after high school graduation. Sitting alone on a creaky porch swing, he'd watched twilight fade into a star-speckled sky, the porch boards warm beneath his feet. He had spent nearly four years in that modest, well-kept three-bedroom house with his foster parents. They had shown him kindness and care, treating him no differently than they did Tim and Mary, the two other foster kids who shared the home. Still, despite their warmth, that deeper sense of belonging, the feeling of truly being part of something, had always eluded him. It lingered just out of reach, like a word on the tip of his tongue.

That night, sitting quietly on the porch with the stars flickering overhead, he came to a decision. Maybe the military could give him what he'd been searching for. Not just a path forward, but a purpose. A place where loyalty, duty, and sacrifice might finally make him feel like he belonged. He understood even then that such a choice could one day cost him his life, but to him, that seemed like a fair exchange for something he had wanted more than anything—a true family.

Now, with the threat clear and immediate, that choice crystallized into action.

The man with the AT4 stood at the edge of the walkway ahead, oblivious to the human missile bearing down on him. Brent watched in horror as the attacker flipped the forward safety into position with a casual flick of his thumb, then slammed the cocking lever home with the heel of his hand. A metallic click echoed faintly above the growing crowd noise. Brent's heart pounded in his ears as he screamed, but his voice was lost in the rising tide of panic as civilians shrieked and scattered in every direction.

The attacker knelt and raised the launcher to his shoulder, lining up his shot with cold deliberation. Brent didn't have to look to know what the target was. The Oval Office loomed just beyond the tree line. The man's right eye pressed against the sight. He took a breath and let it out slowly, steadying the tube.

Brent pushed harder, calling on every reserve of strength as his shoes pounded the concrete. With a final burst of effort, he launched himself through the air, reaching out with his right hand just as the man's finger depressed the red firing button.

His palm slammed into the rear of the launch tube, forcing it slightly downward. The rocket ignited with a violent roar, the launcher glowing hot as the round streaked forward. Brent's momentum carried him straight into the man, driving him to the ground like a linebacker. They hit the pavement with a bone-jarring thud, and Brent rolled away, fists clenched and body tensed for another attack.

Pain stabbed through his right hand like white-hot needles. He glanced down, gasping. The flesh was raw and seared, burned by the scorching blast from the launcher's backwash. He gritted his teeth and ignored it. He'd deal with the pain later, if there was a later.

The attacker scrambled upright, blood trickling from a split lip. With a look of cold fury, he tossed the empty AT4 aside and reached inside his filthy jacket. Brent's eyes locked on the weapon even before it emerged, a black semi-automatic handgun, sleek and deadly. The muzzle leveled at his chest.

Brent didn't flinch. He stared the man down, unblinking.

The attacker sneered and raised the pistol toward Brent's face.

And then, in a burst of motion, the man jerked violently as a hail of bullets slammed into his torso. His body convulsed in a grotesque rhythm, twisting and stumbling backward as red blotches erupted across his chest. The gun dropped from his fingers as he toppled to the ground in a lifeless heap.

As the air exploded with gunfire. Brent dove to the sidewalk, keeping his head and body low as more shots cracked overhead. He crab-crawled frantically across the concrete, ignoring the pain in his hand as he scrambled for cover. A few yards away, a spindly Bradford pear tree rose through a sidewalk cutout. He rolled behind it, pressing himself against its narrow trunk.

Through the chaos, he spotted the Secret Service closing in fast, four, maybe five men, weapons raised, storming toward the downed assailant. Behind them, two Marines lay prone with M16A2 rifles braced against their shoulders. Wisps of smoke curled lazily from their barrels.

A blur of movement to his left. Tony skidded beside him, panting hard. "We've got to get out of here!"

Brent tried to speak but could only manage a hoarse gasp. He nodded, chest heaving.

Tony grabbed his arm and hauled him up. Brent stumbled once, and Tony caught him under the shoulder, half-dragging him into a lopsided sprint. They rounded a corner of the hedgerow, hearts thundering, breath ragged.

Brent glanced over his shoulder. The Secret Service had formed a tight perimeter around the attacker's motionless body, guns still trained on him in caution. One agent crouched and pressed two fingers to the man's throat.

Another agent, standing just behind him, raised his eyes and looked directly at Brent. Then he touched a finger to his earpiece and murmured into the collar of his shirt.

Brent groaned. "Aww, crap..."

CHAPTER 30

A deafening explosion rocked the Oval Office, the blast slamming into the building like a battering ram. The windows imploded in a shower of glass, and the shockwave hurled the President and two secret services agents through the doorway to his private study. He hit the floor hard, dazed, ears ringing with the agents on top of him.

Two Secret Service agents were back on their feet in an instant, nearly before the last shards of glass had even settled. They yanked him upright with practiced urgency and shoved him behind them, away from the open doorway and deeper into the safer confines of the study.

A third agent dropped into position just inside the Oval Office, bracing his SIG P229R against the wooden doorframe, eyes locked toward the Rose Garden. More agents stormed the room, fanning out across the space, weapons drawn, covering every entrance and shattered window, prepared to return fire from any direction.

"All clear!" the agent shielding the President called. "Perimeter team just radioed in. Suspect is down—believed dead."

Lowering his weapon, the agent turned and helped the President to his feet.

"That was close, Mr. President," he said grimly. "We narrowly avoided a direct hit. Looked like an anti-tank rocket. Impacted just short of the tree line outside the Oval Office. The trees absorbed most of the shrapnel."

He paused, then added with a shaky breath, "We got lucky, sir. Guardhouse security spotted the weapon when the attacker pulled it from a duffel bag. They triggered the alert immediately, but we couldn't stop the shot in time. A tourist, a real honest-to-goodness hero, tackled the shooter at the last second. Threw off his aim."

The President straightened his tie and stepped carefully out of the study. Glass crunched beneath his polished shoes. He surveyed the damage in the Oval Office, his eyes moving across the chaos. Secret Service agents were still alert, weapons lowered but still at the ready, their white-knuckled grips betraying how close they'd come to disaster.

Paintings lay strewn across the floor where they had fallen from the walls. Most of the frames were cracked or splintered. Behind the Resolute Desk, the once-pristine windows were in ruin. Some panes were still intact, their bulletproof layers spiderwebbed and sagging inward, while others had been blown out completely, jagged edges glinting in the sunlight.

He turned toward the gaping hole where glass used to be. Outside, shards of shattered trees littered the lawn. Embedded in one of the few remaining windowpanes, a jagged splinter of wood nearly the size of his hand jutted inward like a spear.

He exhaled through clenched teeth. *Should I be scared... or pissed?*

His eyes dropped to a familiar painting on the floor. President Borland's portrait, freshly reframed just last week. It had slid from the wall and landed face-up. He stared at the smiling face for a moment, jaw tightening. Then, without a word, he lashed out and kicked it. The frame cracked apart with a sharp snap, and the portrait skidded across the floor.

Pissed. Definitely pissed.

CHAPTER 31

Charles Roland, Director of the Secret Service, strode into the briefing room, poured himself a steaming cup of coffee, and turned to address the two agents hunched over their laptops. Encased in glass, the Secret Service's Situation Room occupied roughly six hundred square feet at the heart of a much larger operations center. The transparent walls offered both visual command of the entire space and enough separation for secure discussions. Along the perimeter, large computer displays pulsed with real-time data as two dozen agents worked nonstop, updating and monitoring critical information.

"What have we got?" he asked as he pulled a chair out from the rectangular conference table. Turning his chair so that he sat sideways at the table, he crossed his legs and leaned back. He blew across his coffee before taking a tentative sip.

"Well, sir. It seems our boy was an Iranian nationalist, one Mahbod Yaghmaei. Basically, a gun for hire," replied Agent Koffer. "We had him in our database and got a hit on his prints."

"Any idea who his handler was?" Charles asked, already expecting the answer.

"No, sir." Agent Green replied as she closed her laptop and squeezed the bridge of her nose between thumb and forefinger. She was fighting a stress headache brought on by too little sleep and too much time staring at the computer screen. "We tracked a deposit of $500,000 recently placed in his account from a non-existent investment firm and the trail just stopped. We're still running a few leads down, but it's a dead end. Our ambassador is reaching out to the Iranian Embassy to see if they can provide more information on Yaghmaei."

Charles grunted in agreement and took a gulp of hot coffee, feeling it burn its way down his throat. He stood and walked to one of the glass walls, gazing out at the steady flow of people hustling back and forth. *Damn it,* he thought, *all this computing power, people banging on doors asking questions... and we've got squat. Unbelievable!* Sighing, he returned to the coffee urn and topped off his cup before settling back into his seat. "What about the rocket launcher? We're at war. I'd like to think the guy didn't just stroll through TSA with it in his carry-on."

"It was an AT4. A light anti-tank rocket launcher. We pulled the serial number and discovered that it was scheduled to ship to Afghanistan from Fort Campbell twelve years ago but was reported missing during the initial inventory check. At the time, we assumed Afghan soldiers stole it during unloading and later sold it to a terrorist group. Now we know it never even left the United States."

"Anything else to report?"

"We got a lead on the boy that jumped Yaghmaei."

"Really? The President wants to thank him personally. What have you got on him?"

"One of the field agents sent in a report from a..." Koffer paused and glanced over at his laptop. Scrolling down, he found the information he wanted. "... a family of four visiting from Kansas. They stated that they talked to his friend before the attack and that both of them appeared disoriented or possibly sick."

"What good does that do us?"

"They were wearing Naval Academy t-shirts. They distinctly remember it because they asked the friend if he was assigned to the White House."

"Hmmm..." Charles thought, running the possibilities through his mind. "Assuming that he actually attends the Academy, that narrows it down to about five thousand students. But, that's a big assumption. He could be a former student or the relative of a student, or maybe he just bought the shirt because it looked cool." He grunted and continued, "Yesterday, I saw a homeless man asking for change wearing an FBI t-shirt. It's not much to go on."

"I would agree, sir, except we have one more piece of information to go on." Koffer added with a smug smile.

"Spit it out, son. What have you got?"

"Our hero burned his hand on the AT4's tube when he tackled the Iranian. We were able to pull DNA from the skin sample he left behind. I've got the lab running it through the military DNA databases. If he was at Annapolis, past or present, his DNA will be on file. Even if he got the shirt from a relative, their DNA should be close enough for a partial match. That should point us in the right direction."

Charles stood, a faint smile tugging at his lips as he headed to the door. "Well, it's a start. But I'd rather have the entire terrorist network behind the attack. Lean hard on the Iranian ambassador. I'm not going to the President with nothing but a good Samaritan in a Naval Academy shirt. Keep running down those leads and keep me posted."

CHAPTER 32

President Conner glanced up as Thomas entered his office with the head of the Secret Service in tow. "Good morning, Mr. President. Director Roland flew in this morning to update us on the Secret Service's investigation into the attack."

"Welcome to Camp David, Charles," the President said warmly as he rose and extended his hand. Following the attack, the President had left for Camp David while repairs to the White House and its grounds were underway.

"Thank you, Mr. President." The Director responded as he shook the President's hand and then took one of the leather seats at the President's gesture.

"Mr. President, I just came to tell you personally that we identified the terrorist cell that provided the attacker with the AT4. We have neutralized it."

"That's good news. I was told that the attacker was an Iranian."

"Yes, sir. We can't be positive, but we don't believe that the cell has any ties to the Iranian government. We traced the money as far as we could, but the trail went cold. Based on the Iranian government's actions to stay neutral in the war, it would be hard to imagine that they had any involvement. We met with the Iranian Ambassador, who vehemently denied that his government would take part in an assassination attempt on the American President. He's a politician through and through, so who knows? But, we believe him. Moreover, the Iranians had a file on the attacker that the Ambassador, at his government's request, shared with us. That information lead us to the terrorist cell."

"Thank you, Charles." The President rose and extended his hand again, indicating that the meeting was over. "Tell your team I'm pleased with the speed with which they resolved the issue."

As Thomas escorted the Director out, an aide leaned in the doorway and told the President that there was an urgent call waiting from the Secretary of Defense. Thomas locked eyes with the President for a second and then took his seat as the aide closed the door. The President pushed a button on his desk and a display flared to life. The Joint Chiefs of Staff were in the Pentagon's Gold room sitting around a large conference table adorned with the seal of the Joint Chiefs of Staff. Several members were busy typing away at their laptops, while others stood around a large screen showing the coast of Alaska. As the President appeared on one monitors, all activities ceased and the Joint Chiefs took their seats.

"Sir," began the Secretary of Defense. "We found her! The Russian submarine! She's sitting just off the Canadian coast. She's holed up at Prince Patrick Island in Intrepid Inlet."

"Tom, what are you talking about? That submarine has been silent ever since it left port. If it's making noise, then it's because it wants to. This could be a trap."

"We don't think so, sir. They banned fishing in the Arctic, but apparently a Canadian scientific research vessel was collecting samples this morning when something ripped away one of their trawling nets. In that same time frame, our sensors picked up what sounded like a submarine's propellers wrapped in a steel cable. We tracked the sound all the way to Prince Patrick Island, which is at the westernmost of the Queen Elizabeth Islands. Then one of our satellites captured this." A satellite image replaced the Secretary on the monitor. At first, it was just an island. Then, the image zoomed in to focus on an inlet. There, just barely under the water, was the unmistakable shape of a submarine.

A slow smile spread across the President's face. The nuclear submarine was still fully capable of launching its nuclear missiles, but to do so when it couldn't disappear left it open for capture. The most logical conclusion was that they found a protected location that would allow the propeller to be cleared and repairs performed, which could take days, depending on the damage to the props and drive shaft.

"Mr. President," the Secretary of Defense said, reappearing on the screen, "the Joint Chiefs agree. This is an opportunity we can't afford to miss. We recommend deploying the USS Nebraska."

The Nebraska was the Navy's newest addition to its hunter-killer submarine fleet. A fast-attack platform built for dominance beneath the waves, it packed twelve torpedo tubes and carried a hundred Mk 48 heavyweight torpedoes, plus an arsenal of other advanced weaponry. In short, it was designed to be an underwater ass-kicker.

"How far away is the Nebraska?" asked the President.

"It can be in the area within twelve hours. When the Russian sub left the Port of Nome, we started easing the Nebraska up to Greenland to have her ready if the need arose."

"Mr. Secretary," the President said in a firm voice. "Send in the Nebraska."

CHAPTER 33

The MH-53E Sea Dragon—the Navy's largest helicopter—roared through the storm-tossed night, its six rotor blades carving through sheets of rain. Three General Electric T-64 turboshaft engines strained at full throttle, pushing the aircraft hard over the churning sea.

In the cockpit, the two pilots sat in near-total darkness, the only light coming from glowing instrument panels that cast a ghostly green wash across their face shields. Their heads swayed in sync as the helo pitched and rolled through the turbulent air. They'd flown in worse weather—but never with the throttles slammed against the stops.

In the rear, the crew chief kept a watchful eye on the eight men strapped into fold-down jump seats. Even at close range, they were nearly invisible; their black wetsuits blending with the shadowed interior. No bulky tanks hung from their backs; they wore chest-mounted rebreathers, letting them sit upright, calm and still. Four faced four, lining the cabin like bookends on a shelf, their eyes fixed on the aisle. Despite the turbulence jostling their bodies, each man looked relaxed, composed. One casually peeled open a Velcro pocket and unwrapped a piece of gum.

Damn SEALs, the crew chief thought. *Ice water in their veins.*

A low vibration rippled through the Sea Dragon's hull, and the crew chief shifted his gaze to the last passenger who was seated apart from the others by a few empty spots. Dressed identically, he almost looked the part, but not quite. Instead of the SEALs' calm detachment, he stared into the storm through a rain-slicked window, fists clenching and unclenching without him realizing. His face was pale, jaw set tight, and even in the dim light, the twitch of his cheek muscles was clear.

What the hell is a rear admiral doing on a search and rescue mission dressed like a SEAL? Shit. If I lose a rear admiral, I can kiss my pension goodbye.

Jim stared out the window, his dark mood mirroring the storm that battered the sea beyond. *Damn it, what the hell happened?*

The last transmission from the Trumpetfish reported it was surfaced, dead in the water—battered by rough seas, propulsion limited, and its reactor severely damaged.

He closed his eyes and leaned his forehead against the cold glass. *Helen would've been in the reactor room. Please, God, let her be safe.* Drawing a slow breath, he exhaled against the window, fogging the pane.

They'd been inseparable in the months leading up to the stealth system's final installation. Every free moment they'd found, they spent together. Their first night still felt like yesterday. He'd expected nerves, but when she'd moved into his arms, it had felt effortless, like it was always meant to be.

His world shifted in that moment. Until then, everything had centered on his career. Romance, marriage, family were noble pursuits... for someone else. Or so he'd believed, before Helen. Her intellect, her drive, her calm understanding of his relentless schedule all forced him to reevaluate what he thought he wanted.

Not to mention those smoky eyes, that radiant smile... and those legs, he added with a wry smile. For the first time, he believed career and family might actually coexist. And when she boarded the Trumpetfish a few months ago, he was surprised just how deeply he felt her absence.

His spirits had lifted when he deployed to the USS Oscar Austin, the Arleigh Burke-class destroyer tasked with tracking the Trumpetfish as part of the stealth system's test. Equipped with cutting-edge sub-detection gear and ASW helicopters, the Oscar Austin was their best shot at reestablishing contact.

Once the tests were complete, Helen was scheduled to transfer aboard, review the collected data, and fly back with him to brief the Secretary of the Navy. *Now... all he wanted was her to be safe.*

He had known that their time together on the Oscar Austin would be severely limited as Helen and a team of experts tapped by the Navy pored over the data. His role as rear admiral would also have eliminated any opportunity that they might have to steal a few moments together. But he would have gotten to see her. And that would have sufficed.

The Sea Dragon pitched hard, slamming his head against the rain-misted window and jolting him back to the moment. He glanced around the cabin. The SEAL team didn't say a word, but their body language made one thing clear—they weren't thrilled to have him along.

They were trained to handle dangerous missions without distractions, and hauling a rear admiral into a combat zone wasn't part of their playbook. Now, on top of everything else, they had him to worry about.

It had taken the full weight of his rank to get the SEAL team leader to agree. Even then, the man had gone toe-to-toe with him, voice low and furious. Said he didn't give a rat's ass about stars or titles and he wasn't going. Period.

But you didn't become the youngest rear admiral in Navy history by being a shrinking violet. By the end of that exchange, the SEAL leader looked like he'd been verbally flayed and tossed overboard.

Moments later, a team member had been ordered to get him suited up and on board, because the bird was leaving in five minutes, with or without the crazy son of a bitch.

A red dome light began flashing overhead, and the SEALs snapped into motion. Jim watched, fascinated by their precision as they silently checked their gear and then each other's with practiced speed. He looked down at his own equipment, strapped tightly across his chest. Half of it was unfamiliar. *I really am a crazy son of a bitch,* he thought. *But what choice do I have?*

The SEAL leader stepped in front of him, grabbed his harness, and yanked him to his feet with a bit more force than necessary. Jim stood still as the SEAL inspected each piece of gear, then reached for an overhead bar as he was spun around so the equipment on his back could be checked.

When he turned to face him again, the SEAL was watching him closely. There was intensity in his eyes, but not without a trace of respect. "You sure you are ready for this, sir?"

Jim tried to speak but couldn't. Instead, he gave a small, sharp nod.

The SEAL stared at him a moment longer, then gave a slight nod of his own, as if reaching a decision. Only then did Jim realize that until that moment, he hadn't truly been part of the mission. That subtle sign of acceptance calmed him, clearing his thoughts for the first time since he was notified of the situation.

He reached out and gripped the SEAL's forearm. "Don't worry. I can handle this."

The SEAL looked down at the hand, then back into Jim's eyes. There was something different now. A quiet determination that hadn't been there before. *Maybe he had a shot at making it through.*

Without warning, the SEAL balled his fist and delivered a hard punch to Jim's chest. Then he jabbed a finger toward his face and shouted over the roar of the helicopter, "Don't screw up!" He turned and moved down the line, barking orders to his team.

"We're there," a voice crackled through Jim's earpiece. "It's rough. Waves are choppy, and the wind is too strong for us to hover long. We'll get as low as we can, but it's going to be tricky."

"Understood," the SEAL leader replied.

Jim moved behind the double row of SEALs facing the open doorway. Without warning, the door swung wide, and the storm slammed into the cabin. He instinctively stepped back to steady himself as wind and rain lashed his face.

Ahead, a SEAL tossed a square rubber block into the darkness. Before it hit the water, Jim knew a compressed air canister inside would inflate it into a boat. A beacon would activate to help them find it amid the chaos.

One by one, the SEALs stepped into the storm and disappeared.

Jim shuffled forward in his flippers. His turn had come. He took a sharp breath and bit down on the mouthpiece of his rebreather. With one hand pressed to his face mask and the other holding the mouthpiece in place, he stepped into the void.

The water hit him like a wall of ice. Shock rippled through his body. He clamped his jaw tighter and drew a breath of stale air from the rebreather. Scissor-kicking upward, he broke the surface just as a towering wave lifted him into the air. Before he could get his bearings, strong hands grabbed his harness and hauled him into the inflatable boat.

"Well done, Admiral," said a large SEAL with a crooked grin. "We may make a SEAL out of you yet."

Jim spit out the mouthpiece and pushed himself upright. He pulled the mask up from his face and peered into the dark. One SEAL tapped him on the shoulder and pointed behind him. Jim turned and saw the Trumpetfish looming in the storm. It looked like a solid shadow in the rain, unmoving, as if the chaos around it couldn't touch it.

He wiped the rain from his eyes and moved to the side of the boat with the rest of the team. The SEALs had a small outboard motor running, and it pushed them forward through the heaving waves. It felt like forever, but finally, the boat bumped against the hull of the submarine. Two SEALs climbed the slick surface and secured the lines.

Jim shrugged off his rebreather and dropped it with the others. He looked up at the storm, then unclipped the Maglite from his shoulder and pointed it toward the submarine. The beam cut through the dark, revealing the SEALs as they moved toward the nearest hatch.

With a sinking feeling in his chest, Jim joined the line and followed them into the storm.

CHAPTER 34

Helen sat cross-legged on the hospital bed, her chin resting on her knees. It had been less than twenty-four hours since Jim had strapped her into a litter and handed her over to the HH-60H Rescue Hawk hovering above the Trumpetfish. The memory was patchy, fractured by exhaustion and trauma. She vaguely recalled someone shining a flashlight into her eyes, shouting questions over the deafening roar of the rotors. Whatever answers she'd given must have sufficed, because the next thing she remembered was the helicopter spinning into a sharp banking turn and then surging forward with a sudden jolt that pressed her against the stretcher. She felt every vibration in the airframe as the T700 engine pushed the bird to its limit, leaving the submarine and the chaos behind.

Since that moment, everything had blurred together. Doctors, nurses, and technicians surrounded her in waves, prodding her with cold instruments, drawing blood, scanning, testing, questioning. She was frightened, but not just by the exposure. Something in the way the medical staff acted unnerved her. Yes, she had taken a dangerous dose of radiation. She knew that. But the agitation among the doctors didn't seem focused on that alone. Their expressions had shifted from clinical concern to something closer to alarm. And whenever she pressed for answers, they avoided her gaze and rushed off, always with vague reassurances and the promise of more tests.

Lying back on the stiff, narrow bed, she rested her head on the thin hospital pillow and covered her eyes with her arm. The sheets beneath her legs were overly starched and crinkled at the slightest movement. She extended her legs under the blanket and tried to find a position that wasn't miserable.

*
**

Stopping the Trumpetfish's reactor from going critical had only been the beginning of her ordeal. After sealing the core and getting the radiation levels stabilized, she had run directly to the decontamination shower, stripping off her gear as she went. Any modesty she might have felt was obliterated by the urgency of survival. Under the punishing stream of water, she scrubbed at her skin while adrenaline still coursed through her veins. Then came the sudden jolt of the submarine surging forward under full propulsion. She barely had time to register it before the floor beneath her vibrated again, the unmistakable tremor of torpedoes launching from their tubes.

The lights blinked out without warning. Another system failure. The backup generator kicked in seconds later, casting the corridor in a dim yellow hue. Dripping and cold, she pulled on a spare set of coveralls, her hands trembling with haste. Then she bolted back to the power room, still soaked, and joined a team of equally grim technicians in jury-rigging the systems just long enough to reach the surface. Once there, the satellite link reconnected and a distress call was sent.

By the time it was over, her strength had abandoned her. She staggered back to her bunk, unable to balance against the rocking submarine as it rode the surface waves. She collapsed into the blanket, coarse and scratchy, and sat staring at the sterile gray walls in a daze. She had no idea how much time passed. It might have been hours or just minutes, but then the door swung open and Jim was suddenly there—his arms pulling her in tight, his wetsuit soaked and smelling of salt and neoprene. The anguish in his eyes cut through her mental fog. She clung to him, the tears coming fast and uncontrollably. Her entire body shook from the release of tension.

A soft voice broke through the silence. "Ms. Sinclair?"

She jerked upright, startled. A doctor stood just inside the room, flanked by a nurse. He looked apologetic, hands raised slightly to show he meant no harm.

"I'm sorry. I didn't mean to startle you."

"You didn't," she rasped. Her throat was dry, voice cracking. "I mean... It's fine."

The doctor gave a small nod and stepped closer, his expression difficult to read. The nurse, standing just behind him, looked on with barely concealed sorrow. Something in her eyes made Helen's stomach twist.

"Ms. Sinclair," the doctor said carefully, "I'm afraid the prognosis is not encouraging. You received a significant radiation dose. At first, we couldn't assess the full extent because this particular radiation signature is unlike anything we've encountered. When I started asking questions about the source, I was quickly told to stop. No one would give me more information."

He paused, watching her closely. Helen held his gaze, unwilling to explain anything. She had no intention of compromising national security or giving details that could jeopardize the stealth system. *If the Navy wanted it kept quiet, she'd play her part.*

The doctor hesitated, then continued. "I'm sorry, but the exposure has already caused extensive internal damage. Several organs have been compromised. With aggressive treatment, we might extend your life by a year or two, but your system is going to begin shutting down. We can slow the process, but we can't stop it."

Helen stared at him, processing the words. Then she looked at the nurse, whose eyes shimmered with sympathy. Her jaw clenched as she turned her gaze to the ceiling. *Damn. Damn. Damn,* she cursed silently. *How could this be happening?*

The doctor cleared his throat. "There's one more issue we need to discuss."

Helen met his eyes, bracing herself. Whatever he was about to say, she already had a sinking feeling that it would be worse.

He glanced down, visibly uncomfortable. The nurse nudged him gently, urging him to continue. He straightened, then spoke softly.

"Are you aware that you're pregnant?"

The words landed like a punch to the chest. Helen's breath caught. She said nothing, only stared at him as her thoughts spun out of control. It was the one thing she had refused to let herself think about. She had taken the pregnancy test just days before boarding the Trumpetfish but hadn't had time to tell Jim. Her plan had been to wait until after the system tests and then surprise him with the news.

Now that hope was gone. *The baby is gone,* she thought. *The radiation killed it.*

But the doctor wasn't finished.

"As I said, you're approximately two months along. The tests show the fetus is still viable, for now. We believe your body shielded it from most of the radiation, but we can't be certain how exposure may affect development at this early stage. There's no precedent for this."

The nurse stepped to her side and gently laid an arm across her shoulders. The doctor took a deep breath.

"I'm sorry, but we recommend terminating the pregnancy immediately. Your body has been through significant trauma. We don't believe it can withstand the additional strain. I've already scheduled the procedure, and we'll be taking you in within the hour."

Helen didn't answer at first. Her mind reeled from the contradiction. *The baby was alive? Against all odds, it had survived?*

Her eyes moved to the nurse. A wave of fierce protectiveness surged through her, cutting through the exhaustion and fear like a blade. *This wasn't just a pregnancy. This was Jim's child. Their child. A life that had fought to survive even as everything else around her had fallen apart.*

She reached up, took the nurse's hand, and gently moved it away. Then she offered a soft thank you, a quiet gesture of appreciation.

Turning to the doctor, her eyes hardened, voice cold and resolute.

"No."

CHAPTER 35

Tony looked over at Brent, who lay sprawled under an oak tree. It had been three days since the jump to the White House, but Brent was still shaking off the effects. Maybe others could not see it, but Tony could see a slackness in Brent's clothes that had not been there before. *He's getting worse*, Tony thought, the realization settling in his stomach like a stone.

He stood and stretched, clasping his hands and raising them over his head until his back popped. Dropping his arms, he squinted into the noonday sun.

It had been over two hours since he'd met Brent here after morning classes. Brent had sprawled out on the lawn and fallen asleep almost instantly. Even now, Tony could hear his low, ragged snore.

Tony stayed seated, leaning back on his arms as he watched his friend twist and twitch through whatever nightmares plagued him. He'd thought about waking him, but in the end, restless sleep was better than no sleep at all. Brent hardly slept these days.

After two hours, Tony's arms were cramping. He stood and wandered toward the Herndon Monument, gazing up at the 21-foot gray obelisk erected in honor of Captain William Herndon, a man who had become a symbol of honor at the Academy.

In 1857, Herndon's ship, the SS Central America, was caught in a hurricane off the coast of North Carolina. With 101 crew and 474 passengers aboard, he and his men fought the storm for three days. When flooding extinguished the boilers and left the ship helpless, Herndon fired signal guns that drew the Marine, a West Indian brig, to their aid.

He filled the lifeboats with women and children and watched as they were ferried to safety. Then, he refused rescue. Captain Herndon remained aboard with his crew and the remaining passengers as the ship went down.

Thanks to their courage, 152 lives were saved. Herndon's sacrifice became the benchmark of naval honor and the origin of the phrase "a captain goes down with his ship."

"Thinking about the Herndon?" Brent asked from behind him.

The Herndon, Tony thought with a hint of a smile. Brent hadn't meant the actual monument, but the infamous end-of-year tradition: the Herndon climb.

Each year, the Plebes, which were first-year midshipmen, attempt to scale the monument to retrieve a Dixie cup hat placed at the top. Their goal is to replace it with an upperclassman's cover. It sounds simple enough until you factor in one key detail. Before the climb begins, the monument is coated with two hundred pounds of lard.

Success requires more than strength. It takes strategy, teamwork, and pure determination.

"I remember the plan that you and I devised to make us the fastest Plebe class to finish," Tony responded with a snort.

"Hey," Brent retorted as he sat down on the monument's base and leaned back against it. "It was a brilliant plan."

"Yeah," laughed Tony. "And like all grand plans, it lasted until the battle was joined."

Brent laughed with Tony, both recalling the chaos of a thousand Plebes charging the Herndon Monument, convinced their class would beat the legendary one-minute-and-thirty-second record set by the class of 1969.

Tony and Brent had helped organize the effort, dividing their classmates into teams for each phase of the climb. The biggest guys went first, forming a ring around the monument with their backs against it and locking arms to create a solid base. A second team leaned back against them, forming a two-layered human foundation.

Next came the climbers. They scrambled up, placing one foot on each tier of the base to spread their weight. Everything went smoothly—until the third tier climbed into position. Now nearly twelve feet off the ground, they reached for the monument to steady themselves... and grabbed nothing but grease.

One fell, caught by the crowd below. Then two more slipped and tumbled down. At first, it seemed like a minor setback. Encouraged by chants and cheers, they scrambled back up—only to slide down again, their arms and hands coated in lard.

Fresh climbers were called up, but they fared no better. After a few failed attempts, the base teams began to tire and rotated out with new bodies. On and on it went.

They finally reached the top after two hours and twenty-eight minutes. No record was broken, but they weren't the slowest either. That honor still belonged to a class that took more than four hours.

In the end, it wasn't speed that mattered. It was grit and sheer determination that won the day.

"Brent," Tony said after a few moments of thoughtful silence that had followed their outburst. "I was just thinking that maybe we need to focus on finding out why this is happening to you."

"What do you mean?" Brent asked quizzically. "It just... well, it just happens. What's to figure out?"

"But why?" Tony said exasperatedly as he started pacing back-and-forth. "Why you? And why do you jump to those people? There has to be a link somewhere, and I think it is time that we need to find out what that link is."

"Sure, I guess." Brent said, lurching unsteadily to his feet. "Where do we start?"

Tony paced some more, lost in thought. Then he stopped and stared at the monument again, thinking about the teamwork required to be successful.

"By finding Reid," he finally said.

"Reid!" exploded Brent. "Why do you want to bring him in on this?"

"Because this is going to take some real creative research and when it comes to research, Reid is the best."

Brent stared at Tony for a moment, weighing his words and knowing that he was right.

"Well," he sighed, "let's go freak the little Plebe out."

CHAPTER 36

Reid was sitting in front of his computer, fingers flying across the keyboard as he played War-Mageddon, an online first-person shooter packed with explosions, chaos, and digital mayhem. His headset was clamped over his ears, and his full attention was on the screen... until the door burst open.

Tony and Brent barged into the room without knocking.

Without a word, Tony walked straight up to Reid's desk and slid a thin manila envelope across the surface, right next to the keyboard. The tone in the room shifted instantly.

Reid blinked and lifted the mic on his headset. "Hold up, guys. Gotta bounce for a few. Be back later."

He exited the game, peeled off the headset, and turned his chair toward them. "What's this?"

"We need a favor," Tony said. He planted both hands firmly on the desk and locked eyes with Reid, his voice even but urgent. "There's a set of people and places we think are connected, but we can't figure out how. We were hoping you could."

Reid narrowed his eyes. That sounded... serious. He looked over at Brent, who stood leaning against the door frame, eyes shut, like he might fall asleep standing up. Reid had heard Brent hadn't been feeling great lately, but this was something else. His skin was pale, and even from a distance, he looked like someone running on fumes.

Frowning, Reid pushed his chair back and picked up the folder. He flipped it open and took out the first sheet of paper.

Just a few lines in, he stopped cold. He looked up, stunned.

"Wait—what is this?"

Tony didn't answer. Brent still hadn't opened his eyes.

Reid looked back down. This was a mission report. Not just any report. This was about a SEAL team raid at the University of California. Real-world stuff. Classified stuff.

Reid's pulse picked up.

"How the hell did you get this?" he demanded.

"Doesn't matter," Tony shot back, almost too fast.

Doesn't matter? Reid stared at the page, then flipped to the next document. Across the top were the words USS Winston Churchill, underlined in heavy pen. Below that was an entire page of handwritten notes... messy, fast writing, but obviously someone with technical knowledge.

Reid slid the paper back into the folder and closed it. What the hell was going on?

He glanced between the two of them again. "Is this for Brent's senior thesis? Look, I'll help, no problem, but..." He trailed off, looking hard at Brent. "Dude, seriously. If you're this sick, maybe take a break. No offense, but you look rough."

Brent's smile was weak and half-formed, but there was a familiar flicker in his eyes. The same glint Reid had seen many times during study sessions and late-night pranks.

"Plebe," Brent said hoarsely, "don't delude yourself into thinking you're qualified to help with my thesis." He gave a dry chuckle that turned into a small cough. Tony cut in quickly.

"This isn't about the Academy," he said. "This is personal. Off the record. If you don't want to get involved, we understand. But we need help connecting the dots. And you're the best researcher we know, hands down."

Before Reid could respond, Brent doubled over with a hacking cough. It was violent and sudden, and he stumbled forward.

"Whoa, got you," Reid said, shooting up from his chair. He and Tony each grabbed an arm to steady him.

Reid was shocked by how light Brent felt, like his shirt was hanging on a skeleton. His forearm was alarmingly thin.

"Sorry," Brent gasped, finally catching his breath. He shrugged away from their grip and tried to stand upright. "That was… unfortunate."

He reached down to retrieve the folder. "We never should've brought this to you," he said quietly. "It was a mistake. Let's go, Tony."

But as Brent reached for the doorknob, Reid stepped in and put a firm hand on the door.

"Jesus, Brent," Reid asked, his voice low. "You okay?"

He studied Brent more closely under the room's fluorescent lighting. The skin under Brent's eyes was dark and bruised-looking. His cheeks were sunken, and the color in his face was practically gone. His complexion was so pale, Reid could see blue veins threading beneath the surface. Whatever this was, it wasn't the flu.

"I'm fine," Brent said. "Just tired. That's all."

He wiped a hand down his face and tried to smile again. "It's no big deal."

"The hell it isn't!" Tony barked. He stepped between Brent and the door, his frustration boiling over. "We need to figure out what's happening. You saw what was in that file, Reid. Brent's not making this up. We're missing something huge, and you're the only person we know who might be able to crack it."

Brent, clearly worn down, slumped back against the wall, defeated.

Reid looked from one to the other, his head spinning. He had never seen his two friends like this. Tony rattled and intense, Brent fragile and out of sorts.

Tony turned to Reid again. His voice dropped low. "Will you help us?"

Reid didn't hesitate. "Yeah. Of course I will. I always was. You knew that."

Tony exhaled and gave him a grateful grin. He patted Reid on the shoulder. "Thanks. We knew you would. We're just a little... fried."

"No shit," Reid said, shaking his head. A grin tugged at the corner of his mouth. "You're both a mess."

He reached over and plucked the folder out of Brent's hand, then dropped back into his chair and leaned on the armrest.

Without looking up, he added, "Now get him out of here. Make sure he gets some rest. I'll let you know when I find something... and I will."

CHAPTER 37

"**M**s. Sinclair?" the nurse said as eased she the hospital door open and entered the room. "There's an Admiral here to see you."

Helen's eyes widened. It had only been a few hours since learning that she was dying from radiation poisoning and remembering that she was pregnant. Her refusal to have an abortion had stunned the doctor, *but how could she end a life that she and Jim had made together?* The answer was that she couldn't.

But that had been her decision made without Jim's knowledge of the pregnancy. She hadn't even considered how her situation would affect him. *Would it be right to dump this on him? "Hi Jim, I'm dying and pregnant with your baby. Oh, and sorry about ruining your career by destroying a nuclear submarine."*

Tears welled up in her eyes and she furiously wiped them away. A jolt of pain hit her as the sudden movement pulled at the IV taped to the back of her hand in one of the few veins they had found that hadn't immediately collapsed. Following the IV line back to the series of hanging bags, *containing who the hell knew what,* caused another wave of despair to flow over her.

The nurse rushed over to check the IV to ensure that she hadn't pulled it free. "Are you OK?" she asked as she squeezed Helen's hand gently.

Helen managed a weak smile that she was not feeling. "I... I'm not ready for visitors. I just want to rest."

The nurse looked at her and nodded. Patting Helen's hand before releasing it, she said that she would notify the Admiral and quietly left the room, pulling the door closed behind her.

How could I ever put this on Jim?

Helen stared at the closed door, barely aware of the tears gathering in her eyes. *We were only together a few months, and yet... it felt like more. Like it could've been permanent. Like it mattered.*

But it didn't matter. Not now. Not with this.

Meeting me was the worst thing that ever happened to him. Maybe his career could survive the stealth system's failure. Maybe it could even survive the loss of the Trumpetfish. But if anyone ever found out he'd fathered a child with the person responsible? That would be the end. No second chances. No mercy. He'd be court-martialed, maybe even thrown out of the Navy.

And he'd never walk away from the responsibility. That wasn't who he was. He'd take the hit. Let the Navy come for him. Probably resign before they could ask for his resignation—just to protect its reputation. She let out a shaky breath.

No. I won't let that happen. I can't.

There was only one way to keep him safe. *He can't ever know. No one can. The public, the Navy… they can never find out about us. About this.*

The first tear fell, hot against her cheek. Then another. Her vision blurred. *I'll never see him again.* The thought hit hard, sharp, and final.

I love him. And I'm going to lose him forever… because it's the only way to protect him.

CHAPTER 38

Jim stood beneath the broad canopy of a towering pine, his shoulders slightly hunched against the cold raindrops that occasionally slipped through the branches. Water beaded on his Navy greatcoat, but he barely noticed. The wind stirred the limbs overhead, sending down bursts of rainwater that tapped softly against his shoulders.

Across the cemetery, a small group of mourners slowly filed past a flower-draped casket. Each one placed a single long-stemmed rose on its lid before stepping away. The deep red petals stood out sharply against the gray sky and washed-out landscape.

He had stayed hidden under the tree's shelter, watching the entire service from a distance. When the last mourner entered the waiting SUV and the small caravan began to roll out, their rain-soaked funeral flags barely stirred in the wind.

Jim stepped forward, leaving the shelter of the pine and trudging slowly across the soggy ground. He walked carefully, navigating around headstones with quiet respect. As he approached, the cemetery workers, who had just begun preparing the casket for lowering, paused at the sight of him. Grim-faced and soaked, he was clearly here for someone important. They silently stepped back, giving him space.

Jim gave them a slight nod as he reached the casket.

Damn it, Helen, he thought, tears slipping silently down his cheeks. *Why didn't you call me?*

Their last words had been exchanged on the helicopter as she lay strapped into the litter. After getting the rest of the Trumpetfish crew stabilized, he had rushed to the hospital— but had been turned away at her door by a young but firm Navy nurse.

He still remembered the shock of it. A lieutenant, standing her ground against a rear admiral mid-crisis. He had grudgingly admired her discipline. But now, with Helen dead before him, he wished he had forced his way into that room. If he had... maybe he wouldn't be standing here today, saying goodbye.

He pulled off his cover and ran a hand through his wet hair. Just as he replaced the hat, he noticed a thin man approaching quietly.

"Sorry to intrude," the man said in a soft voice, leaning toward him to be heard over the steady tapping of rain on the canopy overhead.

Jim glanced over. The man wore a dark suit with a rosebud and a sprig of baby's breath pinned to the lapel. *Another man in uniform,* Jim thought. *Just a different kind.*

"I noticed you arrived late and stayed back," the minister said. "Would you like me to pray with you?"

Jim hesitated, then shook his head. "No, thank you. I just found out a few hours ago. I grabbed a chopper, but the weather didn't cooperate. I got here as soon as I could."

"That's understandable," the minister replied gently. "What matters is that you made it. Are you family?"

Jim shook his head again. "No. Just... a friend. From a few years ago. We hadn't spoken in a long time." His voice cracked. He cleared his throat. "I always thought there'd be time to mend things. I didn't even know she was sick."

The minister placed a light hand on Jim's arm. He didn't speak further, sensing that words wouldn't help. Instead, he stood with him in silence, offering quiet support as grief overtook the man beside him. Jim's shoulders trembled as he let out a choked sob. The rain continued to fall.

After a long moment, Jim straightened and wiped his face with the back of his glove. The minister reached to his lapel, unpinned the rosebud, and handed it to him. Jim accepted it with a faint nod, then placed it carefully atop the casket with the others.

He turned to leave, adjusting his greatcoat.

"Admiral Conner?" the minister asked gently. "You are Admiral Conner, aren't you? There's one more thing."

Jim turned, puzzled.

The minister unbuttoned the top of his coat and drew out a plain manila envelope. "Helen's attorney read her will yesterday. He gave me this in case you came."

Jim stared at the envelope. His name was written across the front in Helen's handwriting. It was graceful, unmistakable. For a moment, he couldn't move. Then, hand trembling, he reached out and took it.

He walked slowly to one of the white folding chairs under the canopy and sat down. Rain tapped steadily against the vinyl covering above him. He stared at the envelope, tracing the letters of his name with one finger.

The minister quietly excused himself, re-buttoning his coat as he stepped away and made his way through the mud toward his car.

Jim didn't notice. He sat for several minutes in silence.

Finally, he opened the envelope. Inside was a single sheet of folded paper and something small and metallic. Tilting the envelope, he let the contents fall into his hand.

A thin gold chain slid out first, with a brass pendant attached. He turned it over in his palm.

Strength & Courage

His eyes filled again. He had chosen those words for her, long ago. She had worn it every day.

He tucked the necklace gently into his pocket, then unfolded the letter.

> *Dear Jim,*
>
> *I am so sorry. I know I hurt you, but I didn't see any other way. I loved you, and I know you loved me too. That's exactly why I could never let you stay in my life. I failed and I couldn't let that failure destroy your career and everything you've worked for.*
>
> *Please believe me when I say I know you would have stayed by my side, even when news of our relationship broke. The media would have had a field day with it. A*

top-secret project gone wrong, paired with a romantic affair between the rear admiral overseeing the mission and its lead designer. God, I can't even imagine the headlines.

I knew I was dying that first day in the hospital and I couldn't allow you to throw away your life to spend such a short time with me. I didn't want you to watch me die.

I wish we could have had that life together. Truly. But it wasn't meant to be.

The necklace you gave me belongs with you now. Putting it in this envelope was the first time I'd taken it off since the night you placed it around my neck. Even on the worst days, I would close my eyes, hold it, and feel the same warmth from that night. Your kiss on the back of my neck, your arms wrapped around me. Just thinking about it now, I can still feel it.

You probably won't agree with the choice I made. But I've followed your career. You didn't just survive the incident, you rose above it. Now they're talking about you possibly running for office. The country needs someone like you... strong, wise, and committed to something greater than himself. I'm proud of you. So proud.

I wish things could have been different.

Always yours,

Helen

Jim's hand was trembling as he read through the letter a second time. Then he crumpled the letter and shoved it into his coat pocket. Standing slowly, he took the few steps to the casket and placed a hand against its cold, hard surface. "Why Helen? Why couldn't you tell me?" He whispered hoarsely as tears leaked from his bloodshot eyes. "I didn't care what they would've done to me. I only wanted to be with you. Whatever happened, we could have worked through it. I... I should have been there for you."

Looking at Helen's portrait resting on a stand near the casket. Jim stared one last time at the only woman he would ever love. The day seemed to get colder as the rain continued to fall.

CHAPTER 39

Reid set his Monster Mutant energy drink beside his monitor and then reached down and pressed his computer's power button. Almost instantly, his powerful gaming computer completed its startup sequence and was ready for work. Instead of launching Steam's gaming platform as usual, he clicked on the Chrome icon in his task bar to launch the web browser. He opened the manila folder that Tony had given him and thumbed through the papers.

OK, who's first? He thought as he scanned the documents. He stopped when he reached the report on the Mission Bay raid.

LCDR Mitchell: Walk me through the part where you got shot in the leg.

CAPT Lasseter: We had just secured Professor Clancey and Professor Jenner at the College of Letters and Science. I sent a scout out ahead to ensure that the path from the college to the Eucalyptus grove was clear. The plan was to use the trees for cover until Petty Officer Remus arrived with transportation to get us back to the

Zodiac. We had left the boat hidden in the weeds at the Albany Mudflats. We reached the trees without enemy contact and formed a perimeter around the professors. Less than a minute later, Remus pulled up in a gray minivan. As we were loading the professors in the back, I heard what sounded like a metallic click, like the slide of an assault rifle being pulled back. I signaled Pickler and Butler to guard the van while I checked it out. I eased back into the trees and had only progressed about 15 yards when a burst from an AK-47 sprayed rounds all around me. I dove for cover, but one round hit me in the leg and I went down hard. As I lay on the ground, a Russian soldier walked up and pointed his rifle at my head. I thought I was done for when someone suddenly tackled him from behind. The two of them hit the ground, but the Russian was fast. He twisted free and slammed his rifle butt into the other guy's head. While he was distracted, I lunged up and grabbed him around his neck and stabbed him in the kidney with my K-BAR. I remember my leg giving out and his dead weight dragging us both down. Then, I must have blacked out when we hit the ground because the next thing I recall is Lt. Miller wrapping a pressure bandage around my leg. I wanted to search for the person who helped me, but we had to move. I hope he made it. Damnedest thing though, I could've sworn he was wearing a midshipmen insignia from the Academy. Must have been the blood loss causing me to imagine things.

Reid leaned back in his chair and let out a slow breath. It's one thing to be in the Academy knowing that soon you will be on the front lines, but to see an actual report where people are dying makes your guts twist into knots. It makes things more real. You realize that your days of racing across campus and hanging with friends are limited and the realities of war are getting closer all the time. It just makes you think.

He shook himself to break that line of thought and started digging into Captain Lasseter. *What's his hometown? Where did he go to school? Where did he enlist? Where did he get his military training?*

He followed Captain "Timothy" Lasseter's career path as he graduated from the Basic Underwater Demolition/SEAL (BUD/S) school and through his successfully earning the NEC SO-5393 Naval Special Warfare Medic, which would allow him to operate as a combat medic. After that, the trail went cold as his SEAL life began. So Reid turned to social media. Facebook, Twitter, Instagram, and so on. It was soon apparent that Captain Lasseter was not on social media or possibly deleted his accounts once he entered the SEAL program. *But,* Reid thought to himself, *I bet that he has parents, relatives, and friends that are proud of him.* One recent post from the Captain's mother caught his eye.

She had shared a post from a Jeff Miller with the comment, "Thank God you are OK." Jeff's original post was simply, "Had a bee sting me in the leg, but I'll be up and back to work soon."

Off work for a bee sting? Reid thought doubtfully. *Maybe if he's allergic.* Reid mused. But it seemed odd. *What if the family is using cryptic posts to stay in touch without drawing the ire of the US Navy?*

OK, Jeff Miller. Who are you? Reid clicked to view Jeff's profile. No bio and no photos other than an old black-and-white image of a pre-teen kid for a profile photo. *That seems odd. That's definitely not Captain Lasseter's photo.* Reid thought as he compared the image's features to more recent photos.

He opened another browser tab and searched for Jeff Miller. The search returned politicians, athletes, YouTubers, but nothing popped out to Reid as significant. *Wait a minute. The image is old. Maybe I can use that to narrow down the results.*

He added "old photo" to the search, and results showing photography studios inundated the results. *Aauugh!* Reid knew he was on to something, but he couldn't find the right search phrase.

Reid drummed his fingers on the desk and took a long pull from the energy drink. Suddenly, he had a new idea. He searched for "Jeff Miller kid" and... JACKPOT!

The first image at the top of the search results was the same image as the profile picture. Reid quickly clicked on it and discovered that Jeff Miller was the kid's name from the old 1950s TV show, Lassie. *Lassie... Lasseter. Captain Lasseter was using Jeff Miller as a pseudonym for his Facebook account so that he could stay in touch with his family!* A little over an hour later, satisfied that he had exhausted what he could find on Captain Lasseter, he retrieved another energy drink and pulled the next sheet of paper from the folder.

Unlike the official report he had just read on Captain Lasseter, this was just a series of notes scrawled in what Reid assumed was Tony's or Brent's handwriting.

Dawson - USS Winston Churchill - Battle of Wake Island

"What the hell!" Reid exclaimed and sat up straighter in his chair. *The Winston Churchill sank during the Battle of Wake Island three months ago!* Shaking his head, he pulled his keyboard to him and punched in *Dawson Battle of Wake Island.*

Almost instantly, he was looking at photos of one Special Weapons Officer (SWO) Joshua Dawson. Reid selected the first link, "SWO Dawson Miraculously Survives Destruction of USS Winston Churchill" and started scanning the story.

"Special Weapons Officer Joshua Dawson pulled from the sea where he had been clinging to a piece of debris all night."

"... SWO Dawson had been the first to reach the .50-caliber machine gun following the surprise attack and returned fire..."

"... narrowly avoided the explosion from a torpedo."

"... found adrift in the USS Winston Churchill's debris field."

"... lifted to safety aboard an MH-60S SeaHawk launched from the aircraft carrier USS Doris Miller."

"... rescue team members mentioned seeing two other survivors, but by the time they had secured Dawson, they

had disappeared. Additional helicopters joined the search, but they were never seen again and presumed lost at sea. "

Reid started the search using the same process as before, but this time, tracing the life of SWO Joshua Dawson provided no challenge to his researching skills. With no need for secrecy, Dawson's time in the military was easy to track through training records, movements from one ship to another as he advanced in rank.

At 40 years old, he had started his career before the war had started. Interesting that he hadn't advanced to Captain based on his background. Reid thought curiously. *Maybe there is a reason.*

Reid shifted his search to look for any anomalies in SWO Dawson's career that may have prevented his chances for promotion, but after several minutes of searching, he had found nothing that would support a disciplinary action that would have derailed his career path. *Oh well, time to move on.*

The next sheet from the folder was like Dawson's. It was just a few scrawled notes.

Major Harris - copilot - Blackhawk helicopter - Fall of Fallon Air Station Battle

Well, if nothing else comes of this research, Reid thought as he yawned and stretched his arms over his head. *I'll be a cinch to ace the next military battles history exam.*

Then he rocked his head slowly from side-to-side to ease the tension in his neck. *OK, Major Harris. Who are you and what connection to you have to the others?* Reid wondered, as his fingers glided across his keyboard.

Major Colin Harris had the typical naval pilot career. He had mostly flown search and rescue operations for the Navy. Later, he requested a transfer to Air Station Fallon to become an instructor for Combat Search and Rescue (CSAR) teams.

Wait a minute. Maybe search and rescue is the connection. Maybe Major Harris was flying the helicopter that rescued Dawson. Reid did a quick search, but the results were disappointing. Major Harris was nowhere near the battle where the Churchill was destroyed. *Damn.*

Looking back at the spreadsheet that he had constructed of Major Harris' career, he couldn't imagine what connection Harris had to Dawson or to Lasseter. Then he noticed a small anomaly in his data. There was a one year gap between Harris's flying search and rescue missions and when he requested the transfer to Fallon. *What were you doing?* Reid wondered as he typed in a search query specifying the year in question.

- - - - RESTRICTED/CLASSIFIED - - - -

What the hell? Reid retyped the query and got the same results. He tried a few different databases, and every time he hit a wall. They had restricted an entire year of Major Harris's military career.

Reid pulled up his research on SWO Dawson and scanned for any activity records for the same year. Nothing.

He quickly typed in a search for anything on SWO Joshua Dawson for that year.

- - - - *RESTRICTED/CLASSIFIED* - - - -

"Hell, yeah!" Reid shouted as he jumped out of his chair and pointed at his monitor. "I got you!"

Plopping back into his chair with a satisfied grin on his face, he repeated the query for Captain Lasseter, smug in the knowledge that his information would be classified as well... but it wasn't. The only record for a Tim Lasseter that year was his scoring 18 points to lead his high school basketball team to the regional finals.

Frowning, Reid studied Lasseter's birth date and did the math. Captain Lasseter would have been only sixteen at the time... far too young for any military record. Reid sat back, stunned. His hunch wasn't just off; it was completely wrong. The disappointment hit hard, draining him. He leaned forward, resting his chin on his hand, eyes fixed on the computer screen.

He didn't even notice the soft metallic ting of his finger absentmindedly flicking the side of his energy drink can.

Then, suddenly, he sat upright. His eyes locked onto the date he had been searching.

"Holy crap." Reid mumbled. With a fury of keystrokes, Reid pulled up his research on Captain Lasseter and started scanning his notes feverishly. Then, he breathlessly typed in new queries related to the Mission Bay raid. *There! It's right there!*

Reid couldn't believe his eyes. He spent the next hour checking and double-checking his results. Finally, he leaned back in his chair, still in disbelief, and reached for his phone to call the guys.

CHAPTER 40

The President strode into the dimly lit Situation Room at 0300 and took his seat at the head of the table. The Joint Chiefs had already been waiting an hour for the USS Nebraska to launch its strike on the Russian sub stranded in Prince Patrick Island's Intrepid Inlet.

"Morning, gentlemen," he said, accepting a cup of black coffee and blowing across it before taking a careful sip. A few subdued greetings followed. Tension thickened the room.

"Mr. President," said the Secretary of Defense, gesturing to the right-hand screen. "That's the satellite feed. The Russian sub is still in the inlet. We've seen significant activity—likely an attempt to clear a fishing net from the propeller—but our analysts say they're still hours from getting underway. The Nebraska will be in firing position at 0200 island time, 0400 here in D.C."

He turned to the opposite monitor. "We re-tasked a second satellite to monitor the Port of Nome. About four hours ago, a Chinese 903 replenishment ship departed, heading straight for the Russian sub at 15 knots—likely carrying replacement parts. It's escorted by a Chinese 054A frigate, but both ships are slow. No immediate threat."

"Admiral Williamson," the President said, "Who's commanding the Nebraska?"

"John Hollander, sir. Solid officer. Former XO on a ballistic sub for three years before taking command."

The President nodded, then turned to the Secretary. "Walk me through it."

"At 0130 Tango time, the Nebraska will round the northeast corner of Prince Patrick Island and approach the inlet. By 0400, she'll be in position at the mouth. Once targeting is complete, she'll fire four MK48 torpedoes, then retreat to a safe location on the far side of the island. From there, they'll briefly surface to launch a drone and assess the damage. If the sub's still afloat, they'll finish the job. If not, they'll dive and head for warmer waters—where I'll buy the first round."

The President leaned back, smiling. Taking Fallon Air Base was a win, but putting a Russian nuclear sub on the ocean floor would send a powerful message: the U.S. was still a force to be reckoned with. If they wanted allies to push back against the Phoenix Alliance, they needed a show of strength. This could be it.

Time dragged as everyone stared at the live satellite feed. The Nebraska wouldn't break radio silence until the mission was over and she was clear. Suddenly, the screen showing Prince Patrick Island flashed white... then the image returned, revealing a massive plume of smoke rising from the inlet's entrance.

"Dear God," Admiral Williamson whispered. "They weren't clearing the propeller. They mined the entrance. The Nebraska is gone."

CHAPTER 41

Agent Sam Fourte eased his black Ford Explorer into a spot behind a Department of Forensic Services—Crime Scene Sciences Division van. The moment he stepped out, the hairs on his neck lifted. The building in front of him was sleek and quiet, all glass and steel, giving nothing away. But the street told a different story: white DC police cruisers and crime scene vans lined the curb, almost sealing the place off.

Something was off. He felt it.

He pushed through the glass door and entered the lobby. Cold, sterile air greeted him. As he crossed the tile floor, his mind replayed the call that brought him here... if you could call it a call. Thirty seconds. No details. Just pressure.

His phone had rung once.

"Fourte," he answered. The response was immediate.

"Agent Fourte, this is Janice Weissman, Director of the Department of Forensic Services. We need to talk." Her voice was clipped. Tense.

"Oh... okay. Is this about the DNA I submitted? Did you get a match?" He'd reached for a pen, notepad already in hand.

"Not over the phone. In person." Her tone shifted becoming sharper, heavier.

His hand froze mid-scribble. "Is there a problem?"

"Be at my office in one hour."

Click.

No goodbye. No explanation.

Now, standing in the building's quiet lobby, Fourte couldn't shake the feeling that he wasn't just here for answers. He was stepping into something much bigger.

Sam reached into his jacket for his Secret Service badge, but the federal agent stationed at the metal detector waved him aside before he could present it. No words. Just a subtle nod, like he'd been expected.

That alone set Sam on edge.

He walked across the lobby's gleaming marble floor toward the receptionist. Each step echoed sharply off the high ceiling, announcing his arrival before he even reached the desk. The woman behind it looked up with a pleasant smile, but it faltered into something more neutral, almost respectful, when she seemed to recognize him. She pointed quickly to the bank of elevators to her left.

"Agent Fourte, the Director is waiting for you. Top floor. Her assistant will meet you there."

Sam thanked her with a nod and veered toward the elevators. He pressed the button and watched the numbers climb. *This is strange,* he thought as the car rose. *They were clearly told to wave me through. And quickly. Something's up... and I doubt I'm going to like it.*

The elevator doors parted with a soft hiss. A young man in a gray suit stood waiting.

"Agent Fourte?" he asked briskly, already turning. "Right this way."

Without waiting for a reply, he led Sam through a quiet reception area and straight into the Director's office. He barely tapped on the door before pushing it open. Inside, Director Janice Weissman sat behind an imposing desk, elbows planted, fingers laced together. The young man gave her a quick nod and closed the door behind Sam, leaving with the soft click of a latch.

Sam turned his head slightly, tracking the assistant's exit. Then he turned back to face the Director.

She hadn't moved.

Weissman was in her late forties, maybe early fifties. Her shoulder-length hair was pulled back, and a pair of black-framed glasses gave her a studious air. One that matched the résumé he knew she had. Behind her, a row of family photos decorated the desk revealing Weissman, her husband and two young daughters, all smiling. But there was nothing warm about the Director's face now.

"Is this a joke?" she asked flatly, her voice taut with disbelief.

She slid a folder across the desk toward him.

Sam frowned, but didn't move to take it. Instead, he sat in the black leather chair opposite her, holding her gaze.

"I'm guessing there's something unusual in that report," he said calmly. "Given the urgent summons. But I can assure you, I don't know what's in it. All I know is, we collected a skin sample from someone who risked their life to protect the President of the United States. As part of the Secret Service investigation, it's my job to find out who that person is."

A long silence followed, stretching so thin it seemed ready to snap. Finally, Weissman exhaled and leaned back in her high-backed chair. Her tone softened, barely.

"Agent Fourte. I don't know what you've stepped into, but you've got a problem."

Sam studied her face for a moment.

"So you identified him," he said. "One of our witnesses mentioned he was wearing an Academy shirt. Is he a cadet?"

Weissman leaned forward, turned the folder toward herself, and flipped it open. Her finger landed on the top line of the forensic summary.

"Brent Reynolds. Nineteen. First Class Midshipman, U.S. Naval Academy. Orphaned as an infant, attending on a full scholarship."

She peeled off her glasses and dropped them onto the folder with a clatter. Then she leaned back again, pinching the bridge of her nose and closing her eyes.

Sam reached forward slowly, tilting the folder to let her glasses slide gently to the desk. He began flipping through the pages filled with charts, tables, dense text. It all blurred together.

Finally, he looked up.

"Director Weissman, I'm not a biochemist. I don't know what I'm looking at here. Maybe you can just explain what you found that's so alarming."

Weissman lowered her hand and stared directly at him.

"We ran a full workup on the sample you provided. Standard identification, cross-referencing with national databases." She paused. "Besides confirming the subject's identity, the system flagged a match in the military's genetic archive. A paternity match."

Sam blinked. "Paternity?" He let out a short, skeptical breath. "You dragged me across town because someone in the military fathered a kid and never claimed him? That's what's got you wound up?"

His voice hardened slightly. "No offense, Director, but that doesn't sound like something that justifies this level of urgency."

Weissman's expression didn't change.

"Turn to the last page, *Agent* Fourte."

Her voice had gone cold. The line of her mouth was tight.

Something about her tone made him pause. He held her gaze for a beat, then flipped to the back of the report.

His eyes scanned the page. The layout was familiar as he'd seen paternity tests before, but as his gaze landed on the listed father, his breath caught.

His voice dropped to a whisper.

"Are you sure?"

Weissman didn't flinch.

"Yes."

CHAPTER 42

President Conner was sitting at his desk, focused on the document in front of him; scribbling the occasional note in its margins. In the days since the Phoenix Alliance destroyed the USS Nebraska, he and Joint Chiefs of Staff had been expecting a retaliation. But so far, nothing had happened. No counter-attacks, no threats, nothing. The not knowing had created a knot in his stomach.

There was a soft knock at the door as it slowly opened. Charles Roland, Director of the Secret Service, and Agent Sam Fourte solemnly entered the Oval Office. Upon leaving the Department of Forensic Services, Sam had immediately gone to the Director and filled him in on the situation. Director Roland wasted no time in requesting an audience with the President. Within minutes, they had been summoned.

The agents stopped and stood at attention, waiting for the President to acknowledge their presence. As they waited, Sam couldn't help but notice that the office still had that fresh paint smell from the Oval Office's recent repairs following the rocket attack on the President.

"Charles, Agent Fourte. Please take a seat," said the President as he placed the document into a folder and laid it to the side of his desk. "You mentioned that you had news concerning the young man that saved my life."

"Yes, sir," replied the Director. "The DNA tests identified the young man as Brent Reynolds, a midshipman at the Naval Academy."

"That's wonderful," the President said enthusiastically as a smile creased his face. "This is the best news that I've had in a long time."

The President stood and stepped to the window, where he gazed out over the newly replaced Rose Garden. "I need to meet this young man and thank him personally. In fact, the country could use some good news with the way the war is going right now. We should schedule a press conference and let everyone know of this young man's heroics." The President suddenly frowned and turned back to the two Secret Servicemen. "Did you say Brent Reynolds? That name sounds familiar."

"Yes, sir," Agent Fourte answered. "You met him during your visit to the Naval Academy."

"Yes! Now I remember!" exclaimed the President. "I gave him my Distinguished Graduate award for being top of his class." The President clapped his hands and rubbed them together. "This couldn't be any better. This is just the punch in the arm that the country needs!"

"Ahem, sir," the Director said quietly to get the President's attention. "There is something else that we need to tell you. I suggest you sit down."

The President stopped and stared at the Director. Charles was one of the few people he trusted implicitly, and for him to suggest that he'd need to take this information sitting down gave him pause. Without a word, he moved back to his chair and sat down. Staring intently at his friend, he said brusquely, "OK, Charles. Let me have it. What is it you think would bother me so much?"

Charles Roland brushed his fingers slowly across his eyebrows and then ran his hand over his thinning hair as he gathered his thoughts. "Mr. President...," he intoned. "The DNA results turned up another match in the Academy's database. The match was so close that it could only be from...," He paused and took a breath. Then, he squared his shoulders and locked eyes with the President before continuing, "his father."

The President sat silent for a moment and then shook his head slowly from side-to-side as a frown creased his features. "If you're suggesting that the young man is my son, then you are mistaken. You know I haven't even dated anyone in nearly 20 years. Not since..." The President's voice wavered as his gazed shifted to a shelf built into the wall of the Oval Office where a miniature replica of his first command, the Trumpetfish, sat. Draped over the submarine's sail was a small gold necklace with the words "STRENGTH & COURAGE" engraved on its pendant... Helen's necklace.

"Yes, sir." Charles answered the President's unasked question. "Brent Reynolds is yours and Helen Sinclair's son."

CHAPTER 43

Tony's phone buzzed on the nightstand, its screen flaring to life and slicing through the darkness. A few seconds passed before he stirred, fumbling blindly until his fingers closed around it. The glow stung his eyes as he blinked at the screen.

2:00 AM
Reid

What the hell does he want at this hour? He swiped to answer, muttering, "Damn it, Reid... it's two in the morning. Can't this wait?"

"I found the connection!" Reid's voice crackled through the speaker, urgent and breathless. "I don't know what it means yet, but it's there! Grab Brent and get over here. This is big! Huge!"

Then silence. The call ended.

Tony stared at the screen, still lit in his hand, then slowly lowered it to the mattress. For a moment, he just sat there in the dark, trying to decide if this was worth getting out of bed for—or if it was the start of another headache.

Probably both.

With a sigh, he swung his legs out from under the covers, his feet landing on the cold vinyl floor. He yanked open his closet, pulled on sweatpants and a gray sweatshirt stamped with *NAVY*, then slipped into his running shoes.

A minute later, he was easing into the hallway, jogging quietly in the direction of Brent's dorm. As his footsteps echoed softly down the corridor, one thought gnawed at him, *Whatever Reid found... was this the breakthrough they needed—or the start of something worse?*

*
**

Tony and Brent opened Reid's door without knocking and were immediately hit by the glare of overhead lights. The room was ablaze—unnaturally bright for this hour. Normally, three plebes shared a dorm room, but Reid's two roommates had dropped out before signing their five-year commitments, leaving him with the space to himself for the semester.

Reid paced in front of his computer, clutching an energy drink like it was a lifeline. On the desk, Tony spotted a small graveyard of empty cans.

"Damn, Reid," Tony muttered as Brent slipped past him and dropped into the chair at the unused cadet desk. "You keep pounding those, you're gonna have a heart attack."

Reid gave a sheepish grin. "They're not that bad. Just need a jolt now and then to keep the brain cells lubricated."

Tony shook his head and leaned against the doorframe. "Okay. We're here. What's this 'big connection' you dragged us out of bed for?"

Reid's grin widened. "You seriously aren't gonna believe this." He dropped into his chair and began flipping through windows on his computer. "At first, I didn't believe it either. I mean... how could it be true?"

"Reid," Brent said sharply. "Put the can down and focus. This could be important."

Reid froze mid-sip, then slowly set the drink aside. He rubbed his face with both hands and nodded. "Sorry, guys. I've been at this for hours. I guess I got a little... amped."

Tony stepped inside, grabbed the other chair, and joined them in a loose half-circle around the screen. "It's fine. We're here. Show us what you've got."

Reid reached for a sheet of paper beside the keyboard. "Let's start with Special Weapons Officer Joshua Dawson. The guy rescued from the Winston Churchill. I traced his service history. At first, nothing stood out, except maybe his age. Forty's a little old for active duty, but with his background in electronics, I figured they made an exception."

Brent raised an eyebrow and glanced at Tony. "I thought you said you found something."

"Just hang on," Reid said, waving him off. "Let me lay it out. I spent hours tracking this down."

He grabbed another paper. "Next, Major Colin Harris. I initially thought he might have been the pilot who rescued

Dawson because he's listed as a search-and-rescue pilot. But he was stationed at Fallon Air Base when the Churchill went down."

"Search-and-rescue?" Tony asked looking over at Brent. "He was in a Blackhawk."

Reid looked up sharply. "Wait—what do you mean, he was in a Blackhawk?"

Brent jumped in, a little too quickly. "We just read that in our research. It surprised us when you said SAR pilot."

"Oh. Well... yeah," Reid said, faltering. "Blackhawks are often used in SAR ops. Anyway, he did that for years before transferring to Fallon to train pilots."

Still puzzled by the exchange, Reid looked from Brent to Tony, who leaned back in his chair with arms crossed.

"So," Reid continued, "besides Harris being about the same age as Dawson, nothing jumped out... until I noticed something odd in his service record. There's a one-year gap. Completely missing."

"Glitch in the system?" Tony asked. "Someone delete it by accident?"

"Nope. Not deleted," Reid said firmly. "Classified."

That got their attention.

"I tried poking around, but hit a firewall. Serious encryption. That year is sealed tight. If I'd pushed any harder, Homeland would probably be kicking down this door." Then he leaned forward, eyes gleaming. "So I checked Dawson's file for the same year." He paused for effect.

"It's classified too."

The room fell silent. One classified record might mean nothing. Two people connected to the same classified year? That was something else entirely.

Tony finally broke the silence. "What about the other two names we gave you? The SEAL and the President?"

Reid's expression lit up. He looked like he'd been waiting for that question.

"The President's file is classified as well. Or, I should say, Admiral Conner's file. This was back before he took office." He reached for his energy drink, caught Brent's glare mid-reach, and set it back down with a sheepish chuckle. "Habit."

Brent leaned in, his voice low and tight. "Okay. Three records, same missing year. It's interesting, but I thought you had something big."

"It is big!" Reid exclaimed, arms outstretched like he was trying to physically show them the scale. "I'm getting there."

Tony narrowed his eyes. "What about the SEAL? Captain Lasseter. Let me guess—classified?"

Reid grinned. "Not even close. I can tell you everything he did that year including the stats from his high school basketball season. Kid was a star."

Tony and Brent exchanged a look.

"So," Reid continued quickly, "I dug back into the mission file. Lasseter doesn't fit the pattern. But the people he rescued? Different story." He spun in his chair and typed furiously, then swiveled the monitor toward them.

A news headline filled the screen:

Rescued! Two Professors from College of Letters & Science

Reid jabbed the headline with a finger. "A Russian shot Lasseter during the rescue. But the people he saved? They're the key. None of the SEALs were old enough to have served during that missing year. But the professors were."

Tony leaned forward. "Are you saying—?"

"One of them, William Clancy, was ex-Navy. Nuclear engineer. And yes, his record has the same year classified."

"Damn," Brent muttered. "You found the pattern. Now we just need to figure out what happened during that year."

Reid leaned back, clearly pleased. "I already know."

Tony sat up fast. "What is it?"

"Easy!" Reid flinched, raising both hands. "The clue was the President. His profile's too high to hide the truth completely. That missing year? That's when the war broke out. Every single person on this list, including the President, was connected to the same mission."

His eyes gleamed as he spoke the words:

"The *USS Trumpetfish*."

Tony and Brent stared, stunned.

Before either of them could speak, loud banging thundered against the dorm room door.

CHAPTER 44

Brent sat at the long mahogany conference table in the White House's Roosevelt Room, staring at the wood grain as if it might offer answers. The hour-long ride from the Academy to the White House had passed in a blur. After being approached by Secret Service agents who identified themselves but offered no explanation, he and Tony had been ushered into a black SUV and driven in silence.

Across from him, Tony absentmindedly spun a silver spoon in a cup of untouched coffee, his eyes distant. Brent could read the tension in his friend's posture and felt a pang of guilt tighten in his chest.

What have I dragged him into? The only thing that made sense was that someone had identified him during the attack on the President. *But if that were the case, and they thought I was involved, wouldn't I be in handcuffs?*

Still free, he thought, trying to take some comfort in that. *For now.* He began tracing a small dent in the polished tabletop with his fingertip, the rhythmic motion doing little to calm the storm in his thoughts.

The conference room door opened with a soft creak, and a tall man in a sharply cut suit stepped in. He carried a thick folder under one arm. With calm precision, he placed it on the table and extended a hand.

"Mr. Reynolds. I'm Agent Fourte," he said.

Brent rose and shook his hand, followed by Tony, who stood a beat slower.

"Mr. Hendricks. Thanks for coming." Fourte nodded politely, then took a seat opposite them. The subtle creak of expensive leather was the only sound as they settled in.

Agent Fourte rested his elbows on the table and laced his fingers beneath his chin, studying them for a few seconds before leaning back and placing his palms flat on the table.

"Mr. Reynolds," he began, then paused, reconsidering. "May I call you Brent?"

Brent gave a slow nod.

"Brent, I imagine this is confusing," Fourte said, offering a faint smile. "So let me start by assuring both of you—neither you nor Tony are in any kind of trouble." He glanced at Tony, then refocused on Brent.

"That said, I hope you understand we have questions. A lot of them. About the events surrounding the President's attempted assassination... and we believe you might be able to shed some light."

"I'll try," Brent said cautiously, casting a quick glance at Tony, who now sat rigidly with his arms crossed tight against his chest.

"Great." Fourte opened the folder. "Let me begin by saying that tackling a man armed with a rocket launcher is... well, it's beyond brave. The President is eager to thank you

TORN THROUGH TIME – A MIDSHIPMAN'S JOURNEY

both personally. And let me add, on behalf of the Secret Service and the American people, we're grateful."

Brent and Tony exchanged a wide-eyed glance, the corners of their mouths twitching with reluctant smiles. But Agent Fourte's next words wiped those smiles away.

"So, Brent. Why were you and Tony in Washington that day?"

Brent hesitated, eyes flicking again to Tony. "We just... needed a break. Decided to visit the White House."

Fourte nodded as if that made perfect sense. "Sure. Makes sense." He jotted a quick note, then tilted his head. "Odd, though. According to your instructor, you were in class that morning." He picked up a sheet of paper from his folder.

"Here it is—NL435: Peace, War, and Social Conflict." He peered over the top of the page. "Sounds like a real doozy of a class."

Brent remained silent.

"And yet, you went to that class," Fourte continued, "but skipped your remaining schedule to tour the White House. That's not exactly normal behavior."

"It was a rough class," Tony jumped in. "Brent mentioned wanting to clear his head. Just needed to decompress."

"Understandable," Fourte said, his tone shifting slightly. He picked up another document and turned to Tony. "SP434. Nuclear Physics. Also not exactly a light day for you."

Tony offered a shrug. "Not easy."

"Funny. Your instructor says you're brilliant... some kind of engineering savant. She and Brent's instructor both hold you two in high regard." He leaned back, letting the silence build before continuing.

"So. You both attend demanding classes. A little over an hour later, you're at the White House. You save the President's life. Then, without talking to a single authority, you return to the Academy and grab burgers at the Drydock Restaurant. No one hears a word about what you did. That about sum it up?"

Tony opened his mouth to respond, but Fourte raised a finger.

"Tell me something, gentlemen. How exactly did you get to Washington? Footage shows Tony's car never left the parking lot. And Brent—well, you don't have a car, do you?"

Both cadets froze.

"No Lyft, no Uber, no Metro card activity. So?" Fourte smiled, knowing exactly where he had them. "How did you get to D.C.?"

Brent and Tony stared back in silence, panic rising in their eyes. There was no simple lie left.

Before either could speak, the door opened again. A portly man in a dark suit with a gray tie entered, carrying the calm authority of someone used to ending conversations.

"Time to go, Sam. He's ready."

Agent Fourte stiffened. "Director Roland," he said quickly. "The cadets were just about to answer a question. If I could have just another..."

"We don't keep the President waiting. Do we, Agent Fourte?"

"No, sir," Fourte replied, standing and straightening his coat. "We most assuredly do not."

He turned back to Brent and Tony, gesturing for them to rise. "I'm sure we'll finish our conversation later."

CHAPTER 45

The walk to the Oval Office was brief but surreal. Agent Fourte and Director Roland led them down a quiet hallway, past a neat row of couches and chairs arranged into a narrow waiting area. It was clearly intended for those awaiting an audience with the President. The polished floor reflected soft overhead lights, and the muted tones of the decor gave the space a formal, almost reverent atmosphere.

They arrived at the President's outer office, which served as the final gateway to one of the most iconic rooms in the world. Brent immediately noticed two desks positioned before a set of elegant French doors. Only one of them was currently occupied. Behind it sat a woman with perfectly styled hair, her expression focused as she stared at her computer screen. Her back was to the doors, which allowed bright natural light to spill into the room and cast soft shadows across the far wall.

As their group stopped, the woman looked up and smiled warmly. Rising from her chair, she greeted them with practiced ease.

"Director Roland, Agent Fourte—it's always a pleasure." She stepped around the desk and extended her hand toward Brent. "And you must be Brent."

Brent shook her hand, caught off guard by her enthusiasm.

"I'm Jill Stokely, the President's secretary," she said, smiling broadly. "It's so nice to finally meet you. Ever since we learned you and Tony were on your way, the President hasn't stopped talking about the two of you." She turned her smile toward Tony and shook his hand as well. Then, with effortless professionalism, she gestured around the office as if slipping into tour guide mode.

"Welcome to the President's outer office. I'm sure you noticed the French doors behind me. They open directly into the Rose Garden." She leaned forward slightly, lowering her voice like she was sharing a secret. "Not a bad view, right?"

Brent and Tony were too stunned to laugh, but she chuckled anyway, unfazed by their silence.

"Honestly, most days I have to keep the curtains closed. The sun that pours through those windows can be brutal. It heats my back and completely washes out my screen."

She pointed toward an unusual, curved doorway to her left. "That entrance leads to the Oval Office. The doorframe was shaped to match the contours of the room inside." She then motioned to a door on her right. "That's the Cabinet Room, where the President meets with his advisors and the Cabinet Secretaries." Finally, she gestured behind them. "And of course, you just came from the Roosevelt Room."

As she spoke, Brent realized this wasn't just an introduction. It was her way of calming nerves and setting people at ease before they stepped into the presence of the President. It was working. His heart was no longer pounding in his chest like a war drum. He glanced at Tony and saw that he was peering over her shoulder, trying to get a glimpse of the Rose Garden. *He seemed more relaxed too.*

Just then, the door to the Oval Office opened. An older man in a tan suit leaned into the room. His voice was calm and steady.

"Jill, the President is ready for them." He opened the door wider and gave Brent and Tony a nod. "Brent, Tony, I'm Chief of Staff Thomas Conrad. It's a pleasure to meet you both." He acknowledged Director Roland and Agent Fourte with a courteous nod, but made no move to invite them inside.

"Gentlemen, if you'll please wait here. I'll let you know when the meeting concludes." He stepped back into the Oval Office, holding the door open for Brent and Tony to follow.

Crossing the threshold, Tony felt a strange sense of familiarity. The Oval Office looked exactly like it did in the movies. The President's desk stood before a row of towering windows, flanked by the American flag on one side and the Presidential flag on the other. In front of the desk were two straight-backed leather chairs that looked distinctly uncomfortable. Perhaps intentionally so. *Maybe they discouraged visitors from overstaying their welcome.*

At the center of the room lay a large circular rug with the Presidential Seal. Three couches surrounded it in a U-shaped arrangement that created a more casual, conversational space. Tony started to approach the two stiff-looking chairs when the Chief of Staff gently tapped his elbow.

"The President prefers the comfort of the sofas for more personal matters," he said.

"That I do," came a voice from across the room.

Tony turned to see the President enter from an adjoining doorway. He wore a broad, easy smile, and there was a distinct sparkle in his eyes. His walk was confident and unhurried, and his presence immediately commanded the room.

Tony and Brent snapped to attention and saluted their Commander-in-Chief. The President's smile widened even more as he returned their salute and stepped forward to shake their hands.

Tony was surprised by how firm the President's handshake was. For a man of his age, it had strength and purpose. But what caught his attention even more was the way the President studied Brent. He held Brent's gaze a little longer than expected, as if searching for something familiar. Then he turned slightly toward the Chief of Staff and gave him a subtle, knowing wink.

"Please, take a seat," the President said, unbuttoning his coat and settling into one of the sofas.

"Mr. President," said Conrad, "with your permission, I'll be in your study waiting on those reports we discussed. They should be arriving any minute now."

"That will be fine, Thomas. Thank you."

As the Chief of Staff left through the door the President had come through, Tony turned his attention back to the President.

"First," the President said, "I want to thank you both for saving my life. What you did was incredibly brave."

"Thank you, Mr. President," Brent replied. "Everything happened so fast. I'm just relieved you're all right."

Tony nodded in agreement. He couldn't help but notice again how the President seemed to focus intently on Brent. For a moment, Tony wondered if this was about to turn into another round of intense questioning like they'd had with Agent Fourte. Instead, the President stood and walked over to a credenza. He poured a glass of water from a porcelain pitcher, took a long sip, and turned back toward them.

"Look, boys—cadets—I'm going to be straightforward. We identified you because Brent burned his hand on the attacker's weapon. Our forensic team retrieved a skin sample from it. From there, it was simple. Brent's DNA was already in the military database, just like mine."

He paused and took another drink before continuing. "I don't know a gentle way to say this, so I won't try. Brent, the DNA test confirmed that I'm your father."

Brent stared at the President, stunned into silence.

"Holy crap," Tony whispered.

*
**

The President walked slowly back to the sofa opposite Brent and lowered himself into the seat with deliberate calm. He took a steadying breath before speaking.

"I've been rehearsing this moment all day," he admitted, looking Brent in the eye. "But now that you're here, everything I planned to say has vanished. All I can think about is how much you resemble your mother. When I handed you the Distinguished Graduate award at the Naval Academy, something about your face struck me as familiar. It lingered with me for a long time, but I didn't understand why."

He paused, his expression growing pained. "I didn't know Helen had a child. More than that, I didn't know that Helen and I had a child. So the resemblance didn't register at the time."

Brent sat stunned for a moment before speaking. "Could you tell me about my mother?" he asked quietly. "I didn't even know her name until just now."

The President's face lit up with a bittersweet smile as he leaned back slightly on the sofa, his voice thick with memory.

"Helen Sinclair was remarkable. Brilliant. Beautiful. Easily the most captivating person I've ever met in my life. Her mind was extraordinary. She had a presence that made you feel like you were standing next to someone pulled out of the future. There isn't a single day that passes where I don't wonder how things might have turned out if we had more time."

His smile faded as the weight of that thought settled over him. Grief clouded his eyes, and when he spoke again, his voice was more somber.

"But enough about that. Ask me anything you want. I only knew her for a few months, but I'll share everything I remember."

Brent's face drained of color as the realization hit him. Slowly, almost mechanically, he turned to look at Tony, whose jaw was hanging open. Brent then looked back at the President and spoke in a voice barely above a whisper.

"Helen Sinclair is my mother? The same Helen Sinclair who caused the Trumpetfish disaster?"

The President flinched as if someone had struck him. For a moment, he was pulled violently out of memory and into painful reality. He had been reliving the best moments with Helen, forgetting entirely that her name had since become entangled with one of the Navy's most infamous tragedies.

"I'm sorry, Brent," he said earnestly, his voice filled with regret. "I should have handled that with more care. Yes, that Helen Sinclair is your mother. But you need to understand that what happened on the Trumpetfish was a tragic accident."

He sat forward again, the urgency clear in his posture.

"During the submarine's retrofit, a ballistic missile was damaged while being put in the storage rack and its fuel started seeping out. That made the entire missile storage room highly flammable and incredibly dangerous. When Helen's stealth system was powered up for testing, it triggered an unexpected electrical spike throughout the sub. That surge caused dozens of circuit breakers to trip."

He drew in a breath and continued slowly.

"The storage room, filled with vapor from the leaking fuel, was a ticking time bomb. An arc from an overloaded panel caused an explosion. A massive one. It damaged the submarine's reactor and nearly caused a meltdown. But your mother, Helen, stopped the reactor from going critical. If not for her, everyone aboard would have died instantly."

He stood and began pacing, clearly unsettled by the memories.

"The worst part is, the Captain of the Trumpetfish, one of my closest friends, was badly injured in the blast. He wasn't thinking clearly. He saw a Chinese research sub in the area and became convinced it had fired on them to steal Helen's technology. In his confused state, he retaliated. He destroyed that submarine. That one terrible decision sparked the war we're in now. And when he realized what he had done, he took his own life."

Tony had been following the conversation closely, nodding along, but something tugged at his mind. A small, nagging detail refused to stay quiet. Reid had connected everyone Brent had saved through his strange jumps to the Trumpetfish. The professor. The pilot. The special weapons officer. Even the President himself. All of them had been on the submarine. Except Brent.

Tony's brow furrowed as he struggled to resolve the contradiction. *Wait a second. Brent hadn't been born yet. There was no way he could have been on the Trumpetfish. But then...*

"Wait, what did you just say?" Tony blurted out, interrupting the President.

The President stopped mid-stride and turned to him. "I was just saying that it's a miracle Brent was born at all. Helen was pregnant with him during the accident. Her body must have shielded him from the worst of the radiation. I had no idea she was carrying our child. After the explosion, she refused to see me. I thought it was because she blamed me for what happened. But later, I found out the truth."

He looked down at the floor, his voice softening. "In the chaos that followed the disaster, Helen became terrified. She believed that if anyone found out she was carrying my child, it would end my career. She was probably right. But I wouldn't have cared. I loved her. I would've given it all up to be with her."

Tony's eyes widened. His mind was racing. *Brent had been there. Not as a crew member, but as an unborn child. He had been on the Trumpetfish, developing inside Helen as the reactor neared meltdown. Her body might have offered some protection, but Brent had still absorbed an enormous dose of radiation.*

The President sat back down and continued as if speaking more to himself than to the room.

"Everyone on board received a significant dose. The crew. The rescue workers. Me. We underwent treatments for weeks afterward. Most of us fully recovered, but trace levels of radiation still linger in our systems. We're all required to get annual checkups. So far, there have been no cancers or lasting effects."

Tony stood and wandered to the credenza, pouring himself a glass of water. He barely noticed the condensation trailing down the pitcher and dripping onto the polished wood surface. His thoughts were spinning. *The radiation was the key. Every person Brent had jumped to had been exposed. They were all connected by it. But Brent was different. Brent had been in the reactor compartment and received a massive dose while still developing as a fetus.*

"Do you have anything that belonged to my mother?" Brent asked suddenly.

The President turned and pointed toward a shelf near where Tony stood. "Yes. That necklace there. I gave it to Helen the day she boarded the Trumpetfish to begin installing her stealth system. After the funeral, someone returned it to me, along with a letter she had written."

Brent's eyes locked onto the shelf. "May I see the letter?"

The President nodded and walked to his desk to retrieve it. While he did, Tony remained frozen, staring at the necklace.

What if the objects Brent touched, the ones that triggered jumps, had all been present on the Trumpetfish? But that couldn't be confirmed. No one would have kept a record like that. Or would they?

A flash of memory struck him. One of the objects that triggered a jump wasn't ordinary.

"Excuse me, sir," Tony said suddenly. "Did you have your Distinguished Graduate award with you when you boarded the Trumpetfish?"

Both Brent and the President turned to him, confused. Brent put down the letter he had started to read.

"What does that have to do with anything?" he asked.

"Nothing really," Tony replied quickly. "Just curious."

The President narrowed his eyes, clearly sensing something more behind the question. He had built a career on reading people. And this didn't feel like casual curiosity.

After a moment's pause, he answered. "Actually, yes. I did have it with me. I had attended a formal event that day before flying out to the USS Oscar to monitor the stealth trails and still had it pinned on me. When news of the tragedy reached me, I quickly changed so I could join the Seals in the rescue meeting. I remember because the crew chief noticed the medal on my suit jacket and transferred it to one of my pockets. He even patted it and said that I wouldn't want to lose it."

The President leaned forward slightly. "Now it's my turn. Why did you ask about that award?"

Before Tony could answer, the door to the President's study opened. The Chief of Staff stepped in, looking tense.

"I'm sorry to interrupt, sir, but the report we've been waiting for just came in. It's not good."

The President stood immediately. "Excuse me. I'll return shortly."

He stepped through the doorway with the Chief of Staff trailing behind him, leaving Tony and Brent alone in the office.

Brent turned toward his friend with suspicion. "What was that about?"

Tony's eyes lit up. "I think I understand what's happening. I mean, I don't totally understand it, but I know what's causing it."

Brent crossed his arms. "Start making sense."

"It's the radiation," Tony said excitedly. "Everyone you've jumped to had been exposed to the same radiation on the Trumpetfish. It's like you're connected to them through it."

Brent blinked. "You're saying I'm jumping through time because of radiation?"

"Yes. And not just any exposure. You were in the womb. In the reactor room. You were bombarded! The others got hit too, but nothing like what you experienced. It changed you. It supercharged you."

Tony was pacing now, energized by his theory. "And the objects, the ones you touch, they act like triggers. I think it's because those objects were also exposed. If someone had it during the incident, some kind of bond formed. When you touch it, that bond pulls you through time."

Brent raised a skeptical eyebrow. "Then why don't I jump to where they are now? Why always during some crisis?"

Tony stopped and looked thoughtful. He nodded slowly. "Stress. Think about it. Those moments when you jumped, each person was in danger. High-stress events might trigger the object to a specific time because they are bonded with the person. You're not just jumping to a person. You're jumping to a moment when that person was desperate and their emotions were peaking."

Then Tony jabbed a finger into Brent's chest. "But here's the big thing. We know what's making you sick. Radiation poisoning. And that can be treated!"

Tony grabbed Brent by the shoulders, practically vibrating with excitement.

"It's over, Brent. No more mystery. No more random jumps. No more being too sick to get out of bed. And the best part? You have a dad. The President is your dad."

Brent blinked, stunned. Then slowly, his lips curled into a smile. A real one. The nightmare might finally be ending.

He laughed as Tony pulled him into a triumphant bear hug.

CHAPTER 46

The President followed Thomas into the Oval Office Study, the quiet thud of the door closing behind them muffling the chaos outside. He had barely turned when Thomas, eyes wide with urgency, dropped the bombshell.

"They're planning to launch a nuclear missile from the submarine!"

The President stopped in his tracks, staring at his Chief of Staff in stunned disbelief. The words hung in the air like a countdown. Slowly, he turned to face the small reinforced window, drawing in a breath as if trying to steady himself by anchoring to the distant horizon.

"What do we know?" he asked.

Thomas exhaled sharply. "The CIA just received intelligence that the Russians are preparing to fire a nuclear missile from the submarine, in direct retaliation for the Nebraska's strike. Repairs to the vessel are nearly complete. The second the propulsion system comes back online, they're under orders to launch not one, but two RSM-56 Bulava missiles."

The President closed his eyes briefly. "Targets?"

"We don't for sure, but analysts believe there's a 53 percent chance one of the missiles is aimed at Washington, D.C. Given the sub's location and range, it's within striking distance of nearly every major city in the northern half of the United States. The odds point here, sir."

The room fell silent. The President turned, face taut. "Can we trust this intelligence?"

"They're rating it a two."

The President's eyes narrowed. *A level two meant the information was highly credible, though not independently verified. The only rating higher required confirmation from multiple unrelated sources. In practical terms, this was close to the real thing.*

"We have to assume it's true," he said quietly.

Thomas gave a single nod. "We've already got Aegis on alert. Our systems are top-of-the-line, but with a threat this severe, no one is pretending we have a one-hundred percent chance of interception. The only thing working in our favor is that we know the approximate launch point. That gives us a chance. A small one."

The President's arms folded across his chest as he returned to the window, eyes fixed on nothing. His decision to authorize the USS Nebraska's mission had been controversial, aggressive, and, at the time, necessary. *But now? The price was becoming incalculable. One hundred and thirty-four sailors lost with the Nebraska. And now, possibly thousands more if their missile defenses failed.*

"How many more deaths," he said aloud, "will I be responsible for?"

Thomas hesitated, then asked carefully, "Mr. President, what is our response? We need to be ready with a plan... whether we intercept those missiles or not."

The President's jaw tightened. "Assemble the Joint Chiefs in PEOC," he said, referring to the Presidential Emergency Operations Center located beneath the East Wing. The secure bunker was built for moments exactly like this.

Thomas started toward the door but paused. "Do you want me to have the boys moved there as well?"

The President shook his head. "No. Send them to Camp David."

"But if PEOC can withstand the blast..."

"Then PEOC might survive. It was built to withstand a direct nuclear strike. But Washington won't. Even if the structure holds, the city around it won't. I won't take that chance with them. Camp David is remote, shielded, and easier to secure. Get them out of the capital."

Thomas nodded. "Understood."

As he stepped out to issue the orders, the President remained still, the silence pressing in around him. Fifty-three percent. The number kept echoing in his mind. Slightly more likely than not. A coin flip, with the fate of the nation on the line.

He looked toward the ceiling, as the weight of the presidency settled on him.

CHAPTER 47

The door to the study swung open with sudden force, and the President entered briskly. His complexion was pale, and his eyes held the weight of terrible news. He didn't even glance toward the cadets. Instead, he moved directly to his desk and snatched up the phone. His knuckles white on the handset.

"Jill, I need a security detail here immediately," he said in a low, strained voice. "They're to escort Brent and Tony to Camp David right away."

He placed the receiver back in its cradle, exhaled shakily, and finally looked up. Brent and Tony stood frozen, their expressions stunned, as if the air had been knocked out of them.

"I've just received confirmation," the President began, his voice taut, "that the Phoenix Alliance intends to launch two nuclear missiles. Our Aegis systems are armed and ready, and there's a good chance we can shoot them down. But there's also a chance we won't."

He paused, clearly weighing each word before he continued.

"I don't want to believe they'd strike the White House directly. But after the assassination attempt, we can't take anything for granted. I need you both somewhere safer. Camp David offers better protection. I'll join you there when I can. We can finish our conversation then."

The stress in his voice was unmistakable. Brent and Tony heard it clearly. It wasn't panic. It was the stress of a leader making tough decisions.

Brent understood. After learning the truth about the USS Trumpetfish, it was clear now. His father hadn't chased the presidency for ambition or legacy. He had taken on the most crushing responsibility in the world to try and undo a past mistake. He became President to correct a tragedy he believed he had helped set in motion.

It wasn't for glory. It was to make things right.

Brent felt his chest tighten. A wave of emotion surged through him, sharp and heavy. He quickly turned away so that the man... his father, wouldn't see the tears forming in his eyes.

As he wiped his sleeve across his face, something caught his attention. The necklace. His mother's necklace. Resting on the nearby shelf, its metal glinting softly in the room's light. He stepped toward it, his gaze fixed on the pendant.

Two words were engraved on its surface.

Strength & Courage

They felt like a message.

Brent took a breath and turned back toward the President, eyes clearer now.

"Dad?" His voice cracked slightly, but the word landed with force. It was the first time he had ever called anyone that name.

The President blinked and looked at him, caught off guard.

Brent continued. "Did Mom have her necklace with her when she boarded the Trumpetfish?"

The question pulled the President's focus from the looming crisis. "Yes," he replied automatically, his mind still half-occupied with war rooms, missile trajectories, and impossible decisions. "I gave it to her the day she boarded the submarine. She wore it onto the Trumpetfish."

Tony, still reeling from the news, noticed Brent's expression change. His friend was no longer crying. There was a quiet determination in his eyes. Then Brent turned back toward the shelf.

Tony's heart skipped a beat. He knew that look.

"Brent..." Tony said, voice rising with urgency.

Brent reached for the necklace.

Tony launched forward across the room. "No—wait!"

But it was already too late.

Brent's hand closed around the pendant. In an instant, a pulse of blue light erupted from his body, filling the room with an ethereal glow. The air shimmered around him, and with a flash of energy...

Brent vanished.

CHAPTER 48

Brent stumbled, slamming shoulder-first into a row of metal conduits that ran along the bulkhead. The world tilted and rang around him as a deafening alarm—sharp, pulsing, relentless—stabbed into his skull.

WEE-OOO... WEE-OOO... WEE-OOO...

The sound echoed violently in the confined metal corridor, bouncing off walls and overhead pipes until it felt like it was piercing his very bones. He clutched the conduits behind him for support, trying to center himself, but the realization hit harder than the impact.

He was aboard a submarine. Not just any submarine. The USS Trumpetfish. The actual Trumpetfish.

This is insane. His brain reeled as he tried to process it. He wasn't looking at historical photos. He wasn't having a vivid dream. He was standing inside the real USS Trumpetfish, submerged and operational. The air was thick with the smells of oil, ozone, and something acrid—maybe burning insulation.

The wail of the alarm continued as Brent pressed his back against the cold piping and tried to gather his thoughts. His heart pounded, but his mind was beginning to clear. He remembered the reports, the testimony, the de-classified files: the Trumpetfish's reactor had nearly gone critical, the destruction of the nearby Chinese research submarine.

And that had been the match that lit the fire of the current war.

But what if the Trumpetfish had exploded? If the reactor had gone critical and destroyed the sub, the retaliatory strike would never have happened. The war that followed might have been avoided entirely.

In the back of his mind, a cold truth settled over him. He wouldn't survive this. And yet, strangely, that didn't shake him.

Brent had joined the Navy with the full understanding that his duty might one day demand the ultimate sacrifice. Now, somehow, impossibly, he was standing at a crossroads where his death might spare millions of others. He didn't flinch. He didn't hesitate. Turning his back on that responsibility was never an option. He didn't come here to survive. He came to change history. He was his father's son.

Footsteps echoed down the corridor, and a sailor rounded the corner in a rush. Brent barely managed to duck behind a large piece of machinery as the crewman darted past.

"Bill!" the sailor shouted down the narrow aisle. "The coolant pump's running! Fire up the generator!"

A voice answered from the other side of the compartment. "On it! The Captain should have power in a minute!"

Brent's eyes scanned his surroundings with new urgency. Pipes, panels, handwheels. The thrum of machinery. Diesel fumes. It clicked. He was in the auxiliary diesel engine room. They were trying to get propulsion online.

If they get maneuvering power back... The submarine would engage and fire its torpedoes. The war would still happen.

Panic clamped around Brent's chest. He spun, searching the bulkheads. His eyes locked onto a series of electrical panels and a line of manual valves. *No time to waste.*

Reaching into his pocket, Brent pulled out the small folding knife he always carried. He flipped the blade open with a snap and jammed it into the recessed locking dials on the nearest electrical panel. With a twist and grunt of effort, he popped the cover open. Then another. And another.

His eyes darted toward the aisle, measuring the distance to a second bank of valves. A plan formed... desperate, crude, and dangerous. But it was all he had.

Moving fast, Brent slashed the wire bundles behind the first panel, then another. Sparks snapped and cables hissed. The blinking indicator lights on the components flickered once, then died as the power bled away. At the next panel, he yanked down every circuit breaker, slamming his palm against the switches until his hand stung. Alarms shrieked anew. Shouts of confusion began erupting from across the engine room.

"Hey! What the hell...?!"

Ignoring them, Brent sprinted toward the doorway, pausing only long enough to spin several valve wheels into the full closed position. Machinery around him sputtered and clanked. Someone shouted. Another voice cursed as systems failed in rapid succession.

Brent dove through the open hatch and into the corridor, boots pounding against the metal deck. He dashed up a set of steep stairs, his legs burning from the exertion, and ducked into a narrow alcove just outside a dimly lit passage. Pressing his back into the shadows, he forced himself to breathe slowly.

Below, chaos was erupting. The sabotage was working. The engine room was collapsing into a storm of confusion. Brent leaned forward and peered out from his hiding place. Across from him was a small sign mounted above a row of doors: *Crew's Mess.* The smell of coffee and sweat drifted faintly from somewhere beyond. He turned his head to the right, eyes scanning the passage, and saw another placard mounted beside a thick, secure-looking door.

Maneuvering Room

His pulse quickened. That was it. That was the heart of the sub's nuclear operations. If he was going to stop the Trumpetfish, if he was going to finish what his mother started and rewrite the world's future, that was where it had to happen.

He scanned the hallway again. No one in sight. He took a step forward.

Then he froze. A shiver ran up his spine like ice water as a realization hit him. He was about to meet his mother. Not in a dream. Not in a letter or photograph. In person.

And he was going to ask her to help him destroy the submarine. To kill herself. And everyone aboard. Including him. He exhaled shakily and stared at the door. *Time was running out. It was now or never.*

There she was.

Brent stood in the Maneuvering Room, staring in disbelief at the monitor displaying the interior of the Nuclear Reactor Compartment. His mother, Helen Sinclair, was inside, clad in a gray radiation suit, working intently over a massive cluster of valves and control lines. The hum of the reactor, the flickering readouts, and the faint audio of radio chatter gave the moment an eerie sense of being unreal. But it was real. It was all real.

"Come on, Jake. Anytime now," called a voice over the intercom system.

His mom's voice, Brent realized. He startled as he heard an answering voice to his left.

"It's energized. Helen. The solenoid is showing green on the board."

A few moments later, he heard Helen's voice call out again.

"Jake, the right-side solenoid is toast. The power surge must have burned it out. I need to replace it. Shut the hydraulic pump off."

This is it, he realized.

Time to convince her. Time to ask his mother to allow her life's work, the crew she served with, and her own life—along with his—to be erased from history. His eyes scanned the room. There was no radiation suit for him, but then he stopped and almost smiled. *Why would I need one?* The morbid irony hit him. The smile faded just as quickly.

Brent checked the corridor. Jake, whoever that was, wasn't watching. He reached for the reactor compartment door, opened it, and stepped inside. The lock clicked behind him with a solid finality.

"Helen, did you just open the door? I'm seeing a door alarm flashing," Jake's voice crackled over the intercom.

"Why would I open the..." she began, but the sentence died on her lips. She turned, eyes wide behind her helmet, as she saw Brent standing behind her.

"What the hell are you doing in here? Get out! You're not wearing a radiation suit!"

Brent offered a weak, almost apologetic smile. "I don't need one."

"What are you talking about? I don't have time for this! The reactor's going critical, and you're taking a lethal dose just standing there!"

"It's okay, Mom. It really is." He stepped forward, voice calm but firm. "I know you don't understand yet, but the reactor needs to go critical. We need to let it happen."

She froze, confused. Then slowly, she reached into her toolbox and lifted a heavy wrench.

"Did you do this?" she asked coldly. "Did you sabotage the reactor? Are you trying to destroy the submarine?"

"Helen, who are you talking to?" Jake's voice echoed again through her helmet. "Are you alright?"

"Jake, call security. There's a saboteur in here with me."

A pause, then, panicked: "Helen, the door's locked from your side!"

Brent lifted his hands in a show of peace. "Please, take a breath. Just let me explain."

Helen backed up a step, gripping the wrench tighter. "Why do you keep calling me 'Mom'? I don't know you. And you sure as hell aren't my son."

Brent held her gaze. Everything he'd learned about Helen Sinclair, from technical debriefs to whispered Navy legends, had one common thread: she was brilliant. Logical. Sharp. He had to trust that if he gave her the truth, she'd follow it to the right conclusion.

"Helen," he began, voice steady, "you're the designer of the stealth system installed aboard this submarine. President... ah... Admiral James Conner approved the test mission. And the two of you have been secretly seeing each other for months."

Her grip on the wrench faltered. "How do you know that?" she asked, voice suspicious. "You've been following me? Are you with Naval Intelligence?"

"You think I've been stalking you? I'm not here to harm you. And I didn't learn that from following you," Brent said. "James Conner told me. Less than an hour ago."

She laughed, sharp and sarcastic. "Impossible. He's on the surface, and we're three hundred meters down. You couldn't have spoken to him."

"Technically, that's true. I haven't spoken to Admiral James Conner. I spoke to President James Conner. In the future."

Helen narrowed her eyes. "What the hell are you talking about?"

"In the future, the world is at war. It's been at war my entire life. Millions are dead. Cities are gone. James Conner was elected President because they believed he could end it. But the war began right here, on this submarine. You and I can stop it."

"There is no war," she said flatly. "Jim doesn't want to be President. What are you even saying? Are you insane?"

"I'm from the future," Brent said again, quietly but firmly. "Let me prove it. I'll tell you something no one else could possibly know. Something that only you know."

Helen hesitated, wrench still in hand. "Fine," she said with an edge. "Try me."

"You're pregnant."

The wrench slipped from her fingers and hit the metal deck with a heavy clatter.

Her eyes widened behind her visor. "How...? I just found out yesterday. I brought a pregnancy test on board. No one knows. No one."

"I know. Because I'm your son."

Helen stood still, stunned, breathing audibly into her helmet.

"Mom, we need to talk," Brent said gently.

"Talk fast," she said, voice still shaken. "I have to get the reactor stable before we lose control."

"That's what I'm trying to stop," Brent said. "You're going to fix the reactor. You're going to succeed. The power will come back online, and that's the problem."

Helen stared at him. "How is fixing the reactor a problem?"

"Because restoring power reboots the ship's systems," Brent explained. "The moment you do, the Captain regains full maneuvering and fire control. He was injured in the initial explosion and isn't thinking clearly. A Chinese research sub is approaching, trying to offer emergency assistance. But he doesn't recognize it as peaceful. He thinks it's a threat. And he's going to fire a torpedo."

Helen stared, unblinking.

"The Chinese sub was unarmed," Brent continued. "It never stood a chance. When it's destroyed, it sets off a chain reaction. Diplomatic efforts collapse. China, Russia, and Germany form an alliance against the United States. That moment... that one mistaken torpedo... becomes the spark that ignites the next world war."

Helen leaned against the wall slowly, as if the weight of what he was saying had become physical. "And if I don't fix the reactor?" she asked quietly.

"We die. The crew dies." Brent replied. But if you bring the systems back online, the Captain will launch. The war will start. And it won't stop. Not for decades."

A banging came from the door, urgent and muffled.

"They're trying to break through," Brent said, glancing at it.

"They won't," Helen replied quietly. "That door was built to survive a pressure breach. Trust me, they can't force it open."

Brent turned back to her, stepping closer. "Mom... we have to let the sub stay offline."

Helen didn't answer right away. She looked down at her radiation badge, then slowly pulled off her helmet and let her damp hair fall around her face. She stared at the floor, processing everything.

"I wondered what kind of child Jim and I'd have when I discovered I was pregnant," she said, her voice cracking into a dry laugh. "Time-traveling, world-saving hero? Yeah, that fits."

Brent smiled, tears stinging his eyes. He stepped forward and hugged her tightly. She returned it, slowly at first, then with strength.

"I'm sorry, Mom. I'm so sorry."

She nodded against his shoulder. "It's alright. If anyone was going to talk me into this... I'm glad it was you." She paused before asking, "So, ah... Did I give you a name?"

Brent released his Mom and stepped back, wiping his eyes with his sleeve. "Yeah. Brent. Brent Reynolds."

Helen clapped her hands together and laughed. "My father's first name and my mother's maiden name! Perfect!" A sadness returned to her eyes as she looked at him. "So... Brent Reynolds. Are you really sure this will stop the war?"

"I don't know," he said. "But this is our only chance."

Helen leaned back against the wall and slowly slid to the floor. Brent sat beside her and leaned his head gently against her shoulder.

And they waited.

CHAPTER 49

"As a graduate of the Naval Academy myself, I understand just how difficult it must have been to juggle standard coursework while simultaneously tackling master's-level nuclear physics," the President said as he settled into the chair behind his desk.

Tony nodded politely, but his mind had started to drift. He glanced around the Oval Office, eyes moving over the furniture, the artwork, the flags. Everything looked... normal. But something wasn't right. He couldn't put his finger on it. His neck itched—an odd itch, like his skin knew something his brain didn't.

The President continued, "I understand you're developing a new theory that's stirring up quite a bit of interest. Your paper on... what was it called again?"

"Ah, nuclear warping," Tony answered automatically, snapping back into the conversation. "It's the idea that nuclear power could be used to generate a spatial-temporal distortion field. In theory, it would allow us to manipulate both time and space."

"Fascinating," the President said with a smile. "Nuclear warping of time and space. Sounds like something straight out of a science fiction novel. Do you believe it's actually possible, or is this purely a thought experiment?"

Tony hesitated. "I think it's possible. At least… it should be. Right now, it relies on a number of assumptions that hold up in simulation. But it's all just data and speculative math at this point. The major hurdle is engineering. We have no way to constrain nuclear energy into a controlled, directional field. The technology just doesn't exist yet."

"Well, Reid, I suppose that's where your expertise comes in," the President said, turning to Tony's right.

Tony turned, startled to see Reid sitting beside him.

Wait… Reid? When did he get here?

Reid beamed. "Yes, sir! Tony and I have been best friends since I joined the Academy. When the system bottlenecked during early simulations, Tony brought me in to rework the algorithms. I rebuilt the codebase and tripled the computation speed. Those machines were monsters!"

He took a loud sip from the oversized energy drink the President's secretary had apparently found for him. Then, to Tony's horror, Reid reached out and casually placed the dripping can on the President's desk.

Before Tony could say anything, Thomas Conrad, the President's Chief of Staff, appeared from the President's left and silently slid a leather coaster under the can. He gave Tony a brief, conspiratorial wink before returning to his station.

Tony's heart thudded in his chest.

Something is wrong.

He glanced at Reid. There was no doubt, Reid was a genius. He'd surpassed his professors in his first semester and became the academy's rising star in quantum computation. Bringing him onto the project had elevated Tony's research from theoretical to revolutionary. Reid's modifications to the code had allowed the simulation to run without crashing, even under unimaginable complexity.

But something still feels... off.

"Young man," the President said, now looking at Reid, "I fully expect you to be receiving the top cadet award yourself soon. That's assuming, of course, some Navy think tank doesn't snatch you up before graduation."

"Thank you, sir!" Reid beamed, grabbing his drink again.

Tony smiled faintly. Reid would trade a presidential medal for a lifetime supply of Monster Mutant in a heartbeat.

The Chief of Staff stepped forward and gestured to the door. As they stood, the President rose as well and moved to shake their hands.

"It's been a pleasure, gentlemen," he said warmly. "It does my heart good to see young people of your caliber choosing the military. With the decades of peace our nation has enjoyed, fewer cadets walk the path you're on."

Tony froze mid-handshake.

Decades of peace?

That didn't sound right. His fingers moved instinctively to the back of his neck where goosebumps had formed. A small shiver passed through him. It was if an invisible puzzle piece was out of place.

"You know, Thomas," Tony heard the President say as the Oval Office door began closing behind them, "Helen would have loved those two. They speak her language. I can just imagine her pulling them aside for hours to talk about nuclear theory."

Tony stopped cold.

Helen.

Helen Sinclair.

He knew the name. Everyone in his field did. She had attempted to create a nuclear-based stealth system aboard the USS Trumpetfish. The resulting failure caused a nuclear explosion that devastated the Blake Escapement. Her legacy was one of brilliance, tragedy, and controversy.

But what is it about her name?

His stomach churned. Nausea hit like a wave. He doubled slightly, hand pressed to his abdomen. And then he saw his hand.

Blue. Just the faintest hue, but unmistakable.

Suddenly, it all came rushing back. A flood of images, too fast and too bright. Brent. The Winston Churchill. Fallon Air Station. The assassination attempt. Brent grabbing the necklace. The Trumpetfish.

It all came back.

Brent's sacrifice had worked. The war had been prevented. But Brent had been erased.

So why do I remember him? Tony thought, struggling to catch his breath. Then he understood. *Radiation. I must have absorbed some of it during the jumps. Not much, but enough.*

"Tony?" Reid whispered, leaning in. "Are you okay?"

Tony turned to him, his mind still reeling. He saw his friend, bright, eager, brilliant. And for the first time, he truly understood how lucky he was that Reid was still here.

"I'm great," Tony said quietly, a smile breaking across his face.

He turned abruptly and placed his hand against the door, stopping it from closing.

"Mr. President?"

The President's voice came from across the room. "Yes, Tony? Something else on your mind?"

Thomas Conrad stepped toward them, clearly puzzled. "Gentlemen, the President's schedule..."

"It's okay, Thomas," the President said, rising again. "Go ahead, cadet."

Tony stepped into the room. Reid followed, brow furrowed.

Tony hesitated, then asked, "I know it's a sensitive topic, sir, but after the Trumpetfish... incident, what happened to Helen Sinclair's lab?"

The question seemed to land like a punch.

The President took a slow breath. "That's not something people usually ask me about," he said quietly.

The Chief of Staff tried to intervene. "Sir, perhaps this isn't the..."

"No," the President said, lifting a hand. "It's alright." He moved to the edge of his desk and sat down.

"Helen's lab was shut down. Officially, they called the science too unstable—too dangerous to explore further. Most of the experts agreed. I always believed the truth was simpler: they just didn't understand it."

He looked directly at Tony. "Why do you ask?"

Tony's eyes were steady now. The fog was gone. He smiled.

"I'd like to tell you about your son."

EPILOGUE

Jim Conner sat alone behind the massive oak desk, his weathered face lit by the flickering glow of a computer monitor. Shadows clung to the lines and creases of his skin, deepening the evidence of long nights and heavier burdens. Spreadsheets, procurement reports, and fluctuating inventory tallies flashed across the screen as he scrolled through the data methodically, the way a surgeon reviews vital signs before a high-risk procedure. The rest of the room was cloaked in darkness. He preferred it that way. Darkness narrowed the world, silenced distractions, and helped him concentrate with a clarity that bright lights and movement never could.

At least until the silence was broken by a soft knock at the door.

"Come in," he murmured, weariness leaking into every syllable. He pushed back from the desk, letting the chair creak beneath him as he tilted his head and rolled his neck in slow, aching circles.

The door opened, spilling bright fluorescent light from the hallway across the floor and up the front of the desk, cutting through the room's dim calm. Jim winced, shielding his eyes just as Tony stepped inside and flicked on the overhead lights.

"Mr. President."

"For God's sake, Tony," Jim groaned, squinting through the sudden glare. "We've talked about this. I left office two years ago. Drop the title."

"Yes sir, Mr. President. We have," Tony replied with a sly grin, leaning casually against the credenza like a man who had learned how far to push without going too far. "But I've got news."

Jim studied the young man, noting his posture, his eyes, and the barely contained current of excitement running just beneath the surface. He had watched Tony's rise in the Navy with personal interest, nudging conversations behind closed doors, ensuring that certain names were remembered when it mattered. And when a sitting President drops a name, even the highest-ranking admirals take note. Tony had been fast-tracked and he had more than lived up to it. His concepts in advanced nuclear theory were bold, unorthodox. But bureaucracy and budget constraints clipped his wings before he could soar. Jim had seen it coming.

*
**

He thought back to that cold, gray morning—the day after his successor was sworn in. The wind off the Atlantic had been sharp, biting through his coat as he stood in a cracked, weed-choked parking lot outside a squat, lifeless building. The place looked more like a forgotten storage facility than a laboratory that could change the world.

He leaned on the rental car for a long moment, staring at the bleak facade, then fumbled for the ring of keys. The front lock groaned with age as he twisted it. Inside, faint light trickled through the glass entryway, just enough to guide him to a pair of heavy, gunmetal doors. He shoved them open and reached for the switch. The hum and click of aging relays echoed overhead as rows of fluorescent lights flickered to life in slow succession, revealing a cavernous space lined with dormant machinery and dust-covered consoles.

He had never stepped foot in Helen Sinclair's old lab until that day. But as the vast space unfolded before him, filled with potential, steeped in history, and haunted by ghosts, something deep within Jim began to stir. It was a need to honor a memory.

He pulled out his phone.

"Commander Hendricks."

"Tony. Jim Conner."

He could practically hear the snap to attention on the other end.

"Mr. President. Good to hear from you, sir!"

"It's just Jim now, Tony."

"Uh... well... sir, that's not how it works."

Jim chuckled. "We'll work on it. Listen. I've got a proposition—unless you're still gunning for admiral's stars."

A pause. Then: "Sir?"

"I'm standing in Helen's lab."

Silence. And then, "When do I start, Mr. President?"

Tony had submitted his resignation that same day. Walked away from a brilliant career and a promising command track. Eight years in the Navy, the rank of Lieutenant Commander, deep nuclear credentials, and a track record of commanding high-stakes research teams. He gave it all up for something bigger.

That was two years ago.

Since then, the lab had been reborn. New servers. New tech. New minds. They'd renamed it the Sinclair Technology and Research Institute for Disruptive Engineering—STRIDE. Funded quietly, with deep pockets and deeper trust. No one asked too many questions. They assumed it was a legacy project from a former President. An indulgence.

They had no idea.

Jim broke from the memory, blinking as Tony stepped forward, the grin now gone, replaced with urgency.

"Alright, Tony. What've you got? I've got a call in ten minutes with a chip manufacturer still struggling to hit your specs."

Tony didn't answer right away. He stepped closer, his voice quieter now, but pulsing with energy. "It worked."

Jim frowned. "What worked? The particle accelerator? I thought you tested that last week."

Tony shook his head, his eyes gleaming. "No. The Ununoctium. We irradiated it. It's stable."

Jim froze, the air suddenly thick around him. "It's stable? No degradation? You're telling me… one hundred percent?"

"One hundred percent," Tony confirmed, clasping his hands together like a man barely holding back a rush of emotion. "No breakdown, no energy bleed. It's holding."

Jim exhaled slowly. "That means…"

Tony leaned in, his voice low and electric. "That means the theories were right. Helen's equations were sound. We've matched the stability window with our decay timing system."

He paused, letting the gravity settle.

"Time travel is possible, Mr. President. It's not theoretical anymore. We can do it."

Jim Conner felt the weight of history settle on his shoulders. His pulse quickened. His mind, once dulled by spreadsheets and supply chains, was suddenly racing.

Everything was about to change.

AUTHOR'S NOTE

The "REAL" USS Trumpetfish (SS-425)

My father, Jim Wade, served aboard the real *USS Trumpetfish (SS-425)* from 1959 to 1962 as an Engineman Second Class (EN2), which is why I chose to use its name in this novel. The original Trumpetfish was a Balao-class diesel-electric submarine, commissioned in 1946 just after the end of World War II. She remained in service until 1973, when she was decommissioned and later transferred to the Brazilian Navy.

As a Balao-class submarine, Trumpetfish relied on diesel engines to charge her batteries while on the surface, and electric motors powered by those batteries to drive her twin propulsion shafts when submerged.

Over the course of her career, the Trumpetfish underwent two major upgrades under the Greater Underwater Propulsion Power Program, commonly known as GUPPY. She received both the GUPPY II and GUPPY III conversions, which significantly enhanced her underwater performance and anti-submarine warfare (ASW) capabilities. These modifications included higher-capacity batteries, streamlined hull features, and the installation of a snorkel system. The snorkel enabled her to run her diesel engines while submerged at periscope depth, allowing the batteries to recharge without surfacing—an important tactical advantage during long patrols.

The GUPPY II upgrade modernized many of the submarine's original World War II systems. Her deck guns were removed, and the sail (conning tower fairwater) was rebuilt into a more hydrodynamic shape to reduce drag and improve submerged speed. Internal equipment was also overhauled to support longer underwater missions. Later, during the GUPPY III conversion, the Trumpetfish was cut in half, and a new 15-foot hull section was inserted to house additional sonar, electronic equipment, and crew spaces. This extension allowed for the integration of state-of-the-art navigation and surveillance systems, giving her improved detection range and tactical coordination—vital upgrades during the height of the Cold War.

Years ago, I had the privilege of attending a USS Trumpetfish reunion with my father. It was an unforgettable experience. Listening to the crew share stories and watching their faces as they recalled their time at sea gave me a glimpse into a unique brotherhood built below the surface of the ocean. There was a deep camaraderie there, forged in the close quarters and high stakes of submarine service.

The day after the reunion, we visited Patriots Point Naval & Maritime Museum in Charleston, South Carolina, where the *USS Clamagore (SS-343)*, another Balao-class submarine that also received GUPPY conversions, was moored as a museum ship. Walking through its narrow, steel corridor, my father became my tour guide. He explained not only how the systems worked but offered insights only someone who had lived it could provide.

For example, as we passed through the torpedo room, I noticed a set of crew bunks folded up tightly against the bulkhead. My dad pointed at them and, with a familiar grin, said, "Top bunk's best because you can drape your arm over the torpedo for extra room while you sleep." He delivered the line with a blend of dry humor and matter-of-fact confidence that only someone who had actually lived aboard one of these boats could manage.

As we made our way through the cramped passageways, I began to notice that our slow pace was causing a small crowd to form behind us. We tried to squeeze up against the bulkhead to let others pass, trust me, no easy feat in a sub that tight, but they didn't move on. Instead, they simply stood and waited for my father to continue the tour.

If you ever have the chance to step aboard one of these remarkable vessels, take it. You'll walk away with a deeper respect for the skill, sacrifice, and spirit of the "Silent Service." Sadly, the *USS Glamagor* is no longer available for tours. After developing a leak in its main ballast tank, the submarine was towed to Norfolk, Virginia in 2022 for recycling. However, if you find yourself in the San Franciso area, the *USS Pampanito (SS-383)*, another Balao-class submarine is open for tours at Fisherman's Wharf and offers an excellent glimpse into life aboard a diesel-electric sub.

Touring the Trumpetfish was a great experience that I'll always treasure. That day, and the reunion itself, deepened my appreciation for the men and women who serve in the Navy's submarine fleet. Their work is often hidden, silent by design, but essential and courageous beyond measure.

To all who have served in the Silent Service, thank you for your unwavering commitment and sacrifice. Your courage, though often unseen, has shaped history and inspired stories like this one.

— Larry W Wade

ABOUT THE AUTHOR

Larry W. Wade holds a degree in Manufacturing Engineering and spent nearly two decades developing technical curriculum in hydraulics, pneumatics, mechanical drives, rigging, and other industrial systems. His professional background brings a high level of accuracy and detail to his stories. His short story Alice's Closet won Theme of Absence's online Halloween contest, showcasing his love for mixing sharp realism with a touch of the unexpected. *Torn Through Time – A Midshipman's Journey* is his debut novel, blending technical expertise with a vivid imagination for adventure.

www.ingramcontent.com/pod-product-compliance
Lightning Source LLC
Chambersburg PA
CBHW050131120726
47903CB00002B/316